Tempting Little Tease

KENDALL RYAN

Tempting Little Tease

Copyright © 2018 Kendall Ryan

Content Editing by

Elaine York

Copy Editing and Formatting by

Pam Berehulke

Cover Design by

Okay Creations

About the Book

She's the tutor I hired to teach me Italian.

She's way too young for me, but she's also gorgeous, bright, and filled with a curiosity about life that I find incredibly refreshing.

It's fucking adorable.

I'm old enough to know better, but this pretty young thing tempts me beyond belief. And for the first time in my life, I can see myself falling.

• • •

Is this what it's like to be pursued by an older man? The complete confidence, the lack of expectations, the sincerity?

My God, it's exhilarating.

Quinn Kingsley is totally unexpected. I'm moving to Italy in three weeks to teach English, and while I never expected something so real to develop between us so quickly, our chemistry is undeniable.

There's something so sexy about this back-and-forth

he and I share. Flirting with this man is like playing with fire, and I'm bound to get burned.

Io sono attratto da te. I'm attracted to you, he tells me.

But is our attraction enough to get us through the complications of a massive age gap and an international love affair? Only one way to find out...

Chapter One

Alessandra

"Is it done yet?"

Big brown eyes peek over the edge of the kitchen island. The little she-devil is hungry. Her workaholic mother still isn't home, almost an hour late.

"Abbi pazienza, Erica," I respond with a wink, and she rolls her eyes. *Where the hell did she learn that?*

"Speak English, Alessandra!" she says with a moan.

Reflexively, I roll my eyes. *Oh. That's where.*

I'm Erica's full-time nanny. While her mother is at work, I care for this six-year-old firecracker and her tiny baby brother, Ben. Breakfast, book time, playtime, lunch, nap, activity, snack break, and sometimes dinner. This is my life from seven in the morning until the familiar creak of the door at five when Lorraine comes home.

But this is my life from seven to five for only three more weeks.

Tonight isn't the first night Lorraine has been late, and there's certainly no Mr. Riley to fill the gap. That would be where I come in—Alessandra, nanny extraordinaire. Twenty-two years old, fresh out of college, with a degree in the study of classics and very vague career goals.

"I don't want macroncheese," Erica whines, appearing at my elbow.

"Macaroni *and* cheese," I say, correcting her. She sulks off, bored with my response.

I do have to agree with her, however, as I squeeze the artificial cheese into a pot of steaming macaroni. This isn't my idea of fine European dining, but I'm not in Italy. Yet.

As I muscle the paste through the pasta, I can't help but think of my plans to leave all this behind. Not that I hate being a nanny. I adore these squirmy little brats. But taking care of children isn't what I love. What I love is on the vision board mounted on my bedroom wall. Maps and magazine cutouts, pictures of café lights and cobblestone streets, the country's culture and life, all encircling the very best part of all—a plane ticket to Italy. One way.

I can feel myself drifting away as steam from the

pasta rises to meet my rosy cheeks. I'm dreaming of filling my belly with zesty Italian pasta while losing myself in the eyes of an even zestier dark-haired man with long, olive-toned fingers perfect for—

The soft jangle of keys snaps me out of my reverie. The front door creaks open.

"I'm home! God, I'm home, Jesus Christ," comes the yell from the narrow hallway.

"Mommy!" Erica runs into her mom, throwing her little arms around her mom's waist, nearly taking her down and her bundle of paperwork with her.

Lorraine is a powerhouse of a woman, but the bags under her eyes look almost as heavy as the messenger bag slung across her petite frame. Personal budgeting, I've gathered, is her line of work. It must be if she can manage to cover the expenses of two small children and pay me to watch them five days a week.

"How late am I?" she asks, kicking off her heels.

"Don't worry about it, Lorraine, really," I reply.

"You won't believe the clients I had today. . ."

Clients. The word makes my heart slam inside my chest. Lorraine's voice fades into the distance.

Clients…. Why does that word give me so much anxiety?

I open my phone, trying to remember. It must have to do with my new job. I'll be tutoring English overseas while putting my fluency in Italian to good use. More nervous now than ever, I locate my email in-box with quick fingers.

"Substitute Needed" is the title of the email I didn't get a chance to read before Erica nearly broke her neck on the monkey bars earlier this afternoon. It's amazing how a couple of crocodile tears can wipe all other priorities away…priorities like very important emails.

I open the message with a tight swallow.

Alessandra,

One of our beloved tutors, Sal Rinaldo, has suffered a severe heart attack. Upon his recent hospitalization, we are dividing up his current clientele among our other employees until further notice…

Sal is in the hospital? Sal is the dear professor who got me the tutoring job in Italy, bless him. The news hits me like the rush of unfamiliar spices, making unexpected tears spring into my eyes.

Please arrive at 48 N. Broad St. at 6:00 p.m. to tutor—

Wait. Six p.m. As in, tonight? Here, in Boston? I'm not ready to tutor anyone tonight. This isn't what I signed up for. In fact, it's the exact opposite.

"You okay, hon?"

I hear Lorraine like she's in a bubble, far away.

"Yes, yes," I manage to say. "I just forgot I have another obligation tonight."

A downtown location means it's in an office building. I don't have to look at the clock to know that I definitely don't have enough time to go home and change into something more appropriate. Jeans and a cardigan with a big old ketchup stain on the sleeve will have to do. First impressions be damned.

"The new job?" Lorraine whispers. I've given her my notice, but the little ones don't know yet.

Nodding, I throw my things into my purse, abandoning the macaroni on the stove. Maybe I can weasel out of this. Too short notice. Didn't see the email. Down with the flu. I knock excuses off the list one by one.

But this is my very first client. If I get this wrong, the program could withhold my position in Italy. Would they do that? I don't want to find out.

I'm mapping out my route and grabbing my coat before Lorraine offers no more than "Good luck, sweetie!"

"*Ciao*, Erica! *Ciao*, Ben!" I yell up the stairs.

"You mean 'bye'?" a small voice retorts from her sprawl across the top stair.

I give her my best Nanny Monster growl. Erica yelps and runs up the stairs with renewed giggles.

The clicks of my boots on the pavement are in time

with my racing heart as I make my way to the train station. Fortunately, it's just around the corner. Unfortunately, I have ten minutes to get to a location twenty minutes away.

The train rushes to meet me on the platform and the doors slide open. I step in, grab the nearest seat, and immediately open my phone. How can I salvage this?

Please arrive at 6:00 p.m. to tutor his usual Thursday night client, Quinn Kingsley, in intermediate Italian.

Who the hell has a tutor come at dinnertime? I already have this dude pegged: old, crotchety, and single as hell. Quinn Kingsley clearly doesn't have a wife or a family if he's scheduling tutoring sessions during dinnertime.

These are the thoughts that keep me occupied from the station to the building. I reach the steps and glance up from the maps app for the first time. And then up. . .up. . .up. The building climbs to high-freaking-heaven. KINGSLEY TOWER is engraved in bold letters across the gorgeous dark stone.

Kingsley.

I'm tutoring the owner of Kingsley Tower?

Deep breaths. What do I know about Kingsley Tower? Nothing. Well, not nothing. Money. Lots and lots of money. The interior of the elevator says it all with its pristine interior.

I catch my reflection and could cry at the sight. My cheeks are flushed and my hair is windblown. Either I spent the last fifteen minutes in a mad dash, or I just had the best sex of my life. Regardless, this ketchup stain definitely doesn't speak of lots and lots of money. I quickly roll up the sleeves of my cardigan to conceal it.

The doors ding and slide open.

"Hello." A dark-haired receptionist greets me with a tight-lipped smile. "Hi, there," I say before clearing my throat. "Hi. I'm here to—well, I'm here to replace Sal this evening. The tutor? He—he had a heart attack and has been hospitalized. It was unexpected. So, here I am. For Mr. Kingsley."

Her smile never falters. "I'll tell Mr. Kingsley he has a guest," she says unflinchingly, as if an old man having a heart attack is old news. She disappears through the massive wooden door behind her desk.

Thank God. I have a moment to breathe.

I lean on the edge of her desk. Maybe it is old news. Maybe Mr. Kingsley already knows and wasn't expecting anyone to show up tonight in Sal's place. Maybe he'd prefer to reschedule. Why didn't I think of that before trekking all the way here? A cool sensation of calm washes over me, even as my heart still pounds in my ears.

The doors reopen.

"Mr. Kingsley is ready to see you."

Damn.

"Excellent," I hear myself saying.

"Right this way," she says, already opening the door.

"Thank you so much." I've always been polite, if not brave, during a crisis.

The door clicks behind me as I enter the most beautiful office arrangement I have ever seen. Honestly, it doesn't look like an office much at all. It's almost like a penthouse suite, with gorgeous lounge chairs, bookshelves, and the faint smell of leather floating in the air. The windows overlooking the city are enormous, not obscured by an obnoxious CEO desk or "boss man" chair. The city is completely open, spread out before my eyes.

Mesmerized, I walk toward the windows.

"Do you like the view?"

I turn my head. In the corner of the room sits a man behind a desk. I completely missed him as I walked in. The muted shade of his gray three-piece suit is a pleasant contrast with the simple black leather of his recliner.

Most pleasant of all, however, is that this man is the flesh-and-blood embodiment of every Tall, Dark, Shut-Up-So-Handsome magazine cutout on my vision board.

"Originally, the desk was there," he says, removing a pair of metal-framed glasses, "but I prefer to look out a window rather than block the view." He stands, offering me his hand. "Quinn Kingsley."

I walk to him with a smile, extending my own hand. His grasp is firm and soft, and maybe a little demanding. I accept with hidden excitement that Quinn Kingsley is most definitely not old or crotchety. And from the lack of a ring on his finger, he may very well be single as hell.

"Alessandra. It's a pleasure to meet you."

His dark eyes assess me with an air of flirtation. I can tell by the way one eyebrow lifts as he studies my face, and my cheeks flush. *Oh boy.*

"You're from the agency. Where is Sal?"

"I apologize that no one informed you sooner. I'll be replacing Sal for the coming weeks."

He frowns. "I've only ever worked with Sal." He furrows his dark brows, clearly displeased with the prospect of learning from me. This bothers me more than I care to admit.

"I'm afraid he isn't in any state to teach right now," I reply coolly. "He suffered a heart attack and is recovering in the hospital."

This puts my new client in his place, but I immediately feel guilty. A flush of concern flits across his features before settling into an expression I can't decipher, and he releases my hand.

How long have we been connected? My fingers tingle at the loss of contact, and I swallow.

"I'd be happy to pick up where Sal left with you. I'm completely fluent," I say with the confidence of someone ten years my elder. If I'm to be fired before even getting a chance, at least no one can say I wasn't assertive enough.

"I don't doubt that," he says softly.

It eases my anxiety the slightest bit. My gaze wanders to the window, and the skyscapers and winding highways beyond. "This is the most beautiful view," I say.

"I couldn't agree more." But rather than looking at the horizon, his gaze is locked on mine, and there's a hint of a smile on his full lips.

He gestures to the far side of the window, where two sofa chairs face each other. "Let's sit."

I turn and walk before him, acutely aware of my lack of formal dress. My skin tingles with awareness of his gaze on my exposed neck where my hair is swept hurriedly over one shoulder. But when I turn to meet his eyes again, he's looking at the small book laying on the coffee table.

"*An Advanced Student's Guide to Italian,*" I read aloud. "Is this the text Sal has you working from?"

"No." He leans back in one chair as I sit in the other.

"That's more of a prop. Tricks clientele into asking about my interests, makes it more personal."

When he smirks at the word *personal*, I find myself smirking back.

"So, what text does Sal have you working from?"

"None, actually. We mostly just talk. In the language. So, shall we talk?"

That look, the one plastered on his face. All subtle eye crinkles and sexy secret smile. That look has me crossing my legs and curling my toes. This is a challenge.

Okay, Mr. Kingsley. Let's talk.

"What do you like to talk about?" I ask in English. A good tutor knows not to overwhelm a student on the first day.

"*Libri, musica, vita,*" he says. *Books, music, life.* "Mostly *vita.*" He smiles, owning the cuteness of his English and Italian coupling.

"Soprattutto della vita," I say with a forgiving nod. *Above all, life.* "*Parlami della tua vita, in italiano.*" Tell me about your life, I say in Italian, then continue in English, "so I can understand where you are in your lessons." *And understand you*, I want to add.

And so, in his deliciously rich baritone Italian, Quinn Kingsley tells me about himself. He's thirty-eight, older than I imagined. Not a strand of silver in his dark hair, although I imagine a little salt and pepper would only make him more attractive.

Focus, Alessandra.

He co-owns a dating service with his two brothers. He doesn't know much of his family history or heritage, but he's Italian and wanted to learn the language. The language of love, he calls it without a drop of sarcasm.

I smile. He's a romantic. A romantic with some gender confusion with his nouns and shaky pronunciation, but a romantic nonetheless.

I realize he's stopped speaking, waiting for my response. My thoughts finally catch up.

"*Scusa?*" I ask. *Sorry?*

He's quiet for a moment, his dark eyes penetrating mine. "*Io sono attratto da te*," he repeats, and the words linger in the air between us. *I'm attracted to you.*

What do you say to that?

"You're uncomfortable." He's speaking in English now, genuinely concerned. "Why? Surely, men tell you this every day."

Is this what it's like to be flirted with by an older man? The complete confidence, the lack of expectation of compliment in return, the sincerity?

My God, it's exhilarating.

"No," I manage to say, also in English. "Honestly, you're the first. . .this week."

We both chuckle at my blatant exaggeration.

"Certainly," he responds, and there isn't a drop of condescension in his voice.

I like that he allows my fib. There's something so sexy about this back and forth. It's like playing with fire, letting the oil spit a little before settling in the pan. I uncross my legs, hoping to alleviate the tension building there.

"You're very forward, Mr. Kingsley. I don't experience that often," I say, my tone suggesting something more than observation. I think I'm flirting.

But I'm also being honest. I hardly have a social life these days, and don't meet many men. Certainly none as dashingly handsome and confident as the man seated before me.

He leans forward, his suit jacket pulling attractively against his torso, and I hold my breath. "It's Quinn, please. And, Alessandra," he whispers softly an Italian phrase I have to mull over for just a second.

The laughter that breaks the quiet isn't recognizably mine until I cover my mouth.

"I'm sorry," I whisper with a hidden grin, "but you just said you wish to breed with me."

"Oh, shit," he murmurs under his breath. "You can guess that Sal and I never really exchanged such words. I suppose I need the practice."

"Well, I'd be happy to make up for any lack in your education so far." *What am I doing?*

"I look forward to it," Quinn says and pushes to his feet.

He offers his hand to me, and I accept the gesture greedily. We stand like that, hand in hand, for longer than a courtesy.

"Our time is up."

He can't be right, can he?

"Really?" I say, like Erica when I tell her it's time for bed. I cringe at how young I must seem to him, and he smiles. And that's when I remember that I was late tonight.

"Perhaps we could make up for the time lost over dinner tomorrow."

Despite his consistent forwardness, the invitation still sneaks upon me as a surprise. I open my mouth to respond, yet all that comes out is a soft whimper as I try to compose myself. The way he tilts his head to watch me has me tingling all over.

"Alessandra," he says, and when he says my name, I nearly drop dead. "How old are you?"

Ah. The fun's over now. I remove my fingers from his warm, open palm.

"Twenty-two," I respond, all business. *Good-bye, my sweet flirtation. It was lovely.*

"Jesus," he says, scrubbing a hand through his hair.

Is that the glow of the sunset warming his cheeks or a faint blush? Maybe this doesn't have to end so soon after all.

"I like how you put yourself out there," I say to reassure him. "It's refreshing. New."

His gaze flits back to mine. I was staring, wasn't I?

"How long has it been since you asked a gi—a woman," I say quickly, correcting myself, "on a date?"

"A long while." There's no shame in his voice. Just something like loneliness.

I turn away from our spot near the window and approach his desk. Picking up a pen, I jot my phone number on a notepad sitting in the open. "Last time I gave a guy my number, he sent me nothing but unwarranted pictures." I feel him standing behind me, maybe inches between us, and I turn around to meet his gaze.

"I would never give you anything you didn't ask for."

Holy hell. "Text me if you're serious about continuing lessons with me. And I'll think about dinner."

"I will. *Ciao*, Alessandra."

"*Ciao*." With that, I walk out of the office, my boots tapping on the marble floors past reception and into the elevator.

I stand tall until the doors close, at which moment I melt into a puddle. My red-hot cheeks glow in the elevator's mirrored wall, and goose bumps race up and down my arms. It takes a moment to regain feeling in my fingertips, but when I do, I rub them against my lips.

I'm hungry, starving, and I didn't know it until it was right in front of me.

Until *he* was right in front of me.

I survived this round, but would I manage an entire meal with this man? His intensity is contagious, but can I keep up? He has sixteen years on me.

On me. What would it feel like to have Quinn Kingsley on me?

. . .

"I bet he's experienced as hell."

My friend Deanna knows exactly where my mind has traveled. We're sitting in a corner of our favorite bar, tucked away where we can whisper our dark secrets over Moscow mules. Tonight, she told me about her latest sexcapade with a coworker. In return, I told her the whole story of Quinn Kingsley.

She takes a dainty little sip of her drink, her eyebrows waggling. "And I don't mean in Italian."

"Oh, my God." I groan, dropping my head into my hands with every kind of frustration imaginable. Namely sexual.

"Come on. What are you so panicked about? A sexy, wealthy older manwants to take you on a date. Or—wait—did I totally misinterpret this story? He's sexy, right? Not creepy? Am I already drunk?"

I laugh. "No. He isn't creepy. The opposite, actually. I feel like the creepy one."

"Why?" Deanna whispers, scandalized. "Did you, like, get caught ogling his package?"

"No." I laugh again, taking a sip. "He's my student. Isn't there supposed to be a decorum between teacher and student?"

"Like what? Thou shalt not fuck?"

"Deanna!" I never know what this girl is going to say in public.

"Aly, you're both adults, and you're leaving in a few weeks. Live a little. But don't live so much that you don't spend any more time with me, ya feel?"

Smiling, I take her hand. "Yeah. I feel."

And, boy, do I ever.

Chapter Two

Quinn

Tempting.

So. Fucking. Tempting.

And sweet. And innocent. And gorgeous.

I should stop my brain from cataloging all these thoughts about my twenty-two-year-old Italian tutor, but where would the fun be in that?

I've yet to get any actual work done this morning, because all my brain wants to do is focus on the woman whose scent still lingers lightly in my office from the night before.

But, Jesus, she's twenty-fucking-two.

My lesson with Alessandra was anything but expected. I've been meeting with Sal once a week for a year. Learning Italian has been part of my plan to capture some of my family's heritage. With both of my parents out of the picture, the way we grew up, there wasn't time for discussing the family tree or swapping stories on genealogy. And now that I'm older and have more time on my hands, I find it's something that interests me. And since I know my mother was Italian, it was a logical place to start. I figured I'd learn a little of the language and eventually take a trip there, immerse myself in the culture.

But meeting Alessandra? Swapping flirty remarks in a foreign tongue? It's been the most exhilarating part of my new little hobby. By far.

Rising from my office chair, I take a deep breath and stretch my shoulders. *Fuck it.* Work can wait. It's not like I'm getting anything done anyway. Strolling around my desk, I stop in front of it and look down at the notepad with Alessandra's neat handwriting. Inspired, I grab my cell phone and begin a new message.

Buongiorno, bellissima, I type and hit ENTER. It means *good morning, beautiful.*

I don't have to wait long for her reply.

Hello, Mr. Kingsley. ;)

The formality she's used in combination with the winking-face emoticon makes me smile. She's so adorably young. God, the things I could teach her. Suddenly, I'm hit with an image of her on her knees before me, those wide brown eyes looking adoringly up at me as her fingers timidly fumble with my belt.

My cock gives a twitch behind my zipper, encouraging the naughty little daydream.

Instead of giving in, I take a deep breath to clear my head and type a reply.

Have you given my proposal more thought? I'd love to take you to this great little Italian place I know.

As I wait for her reply, I wonder if there's some sort of protocol I should be following. I know there's something about waiting three days before calling, but I never really learned the rules on dating. Even worse, though, is the thought that she may be the type to play games or blow me off. Alessandra and I are a generation apart. I tend to wear my emotions on my sleeve, preferring to say plainly what I want and go for it.

But then her reply comes in. *Sounds great. When were you thinking?*

Are you free tonight? I type.

It's Friday night, and as soon as I click SEND, I could

kick myself. Of course she'll have plans. She probably has a healthy and thriving social calendar—unlike me. My brothers tease me endlessly about the fact that I'm a homebody.

My phone buzzes in my hand, and I take a deep, steadying breath as I glance down at Alessandra's reply.

Yes, I am. Just let me know the time and place, and I'll meet you.

My heart rate bumps up a notch as I type out the address and hit ENTER.

In this moment, I know two things for certain. One, my evening just got a whole lot more interesting, and two, I won't be getting a bit of work done today.

• • •

I arrive at the restaurant a few minutes early, wanting to greet Francisco, the owner, and ensure my reservation is set. This is one of the most popular restaurants downtown, and I had to work my connections to secure us a table on such late notice.

"The eldest Kingsley." Francisco grins and takes my hand, pumping it up and down.

He doesn't say it, but I know he's appraising me, wondering why it's me here on a date rather than Gavin or Cooper. To say I'm rusty would be an understatement. I haven't dated in God knows how long.

"Table for one?" he asks.

I give my head a shake, and that's when I see her near the hostess station.

Alessandra. She's here.

She looks stunning, wearing a simple black skirt paired with a fitted white top. A delicate gold necklace rests against her collarbone. Her long hair is curled over one shoulder. She looks unsure, slightly nervous. Her mouth is painted the most distracting shade of berry, and I find I want to kiss her like I've never wanted anything in my entire life.

I take a deep breath and force myself to relax.

"Alessandra," I say, approaching where she stands. "You made it."

She bites her lip and then flashes me a grin. Her gaze travels along the front of my torso, and I'm suddenly thankful for all the extra hours I spend in the gym.

"Mr. Kingsley," she says, her mouth curving into a full-on smile now. It's so bright and transformative, it takes over her entire face, lighting up her eyes and making my knees weak.

I take her hand and lift it to my mouth, pressing a soft kiss to the back of it. This small gesture seems to mean something to her, and I'm hopeful my manners and charm make up for the fact that she's totally and completely out of my league.

"Call me Quinn," I correct her.

Francisco clears his throat next to me. I'm not sure when he approached, but his look is bemused as he watches me with Alessandra.

It's then that I realize how absurd this is—her and me.

She's barely legal, so supple and fresh. *Jesus.* I want her like I've never desired another woman in my entire life. Even though I know we make no sense, I realize I'm committed to seeing this through. The thought of bantering with her in Italian is almost as intoxicating as the thought of having her in my bed.

"Table for two," Francisco says. "Right this way."

Alessandra and I are seated and order a bottle of merlot from our waitress. When it's delivered and uncorked, I raise my glass to hers.

"Cheers," I murmur.

"To?" she asks, her eyes flashing on mine seductively.

"Would it be too cheesy if I said 'to getting to know each other better'?"

She laughs, the sound lively and uninhibited. "A little, but I'll admit, I like that idea, too."

"Good. Because I'd like nothing more."

"All right, then." She translates our toast in Italian and in that moment, I'm speechless. Everything feels so surreal in that moment and I can't take my eyes off of her. Who is this vixen who has my mind so tangled up? I just sit there and stare at her, her glass raised as she awaits my response.

I'm only able to respond back with, "*Saluti.*"

We peruse the menu and make small talk. I'm curious

to know how she ended up studying Italian.

She shrugs, looking contemplatively into her wineglass. "Huge Italian family. I guess you could say I've been studying it since I was born. But then in college, I began my more formal education in the language, fully immersing myself in the history with courses taught completely in Italian, a full immersion program without actually being in Italy, which was great because then I was able to converse more deeply with my grandmother before she passed two years ago."

"I'm sorry." I reach over and take her hand, giving it a squeeze.

"She was eighty-six and had lived a great life. We should all be so lucky."

At this, we both lift our glasses and drink.

"What about you?" she asks. "Tell me about your family. Are you from Boston?"

"Born and raised. Last year, I became interested in studying my ancestry, and since I knew my mother's family was Italian, I sort of fell into it. I began studying the language, even took a cooking class on Tuscan techniques, and I'm looking forward to traveling there soon, too."

Alessandra nods. "I think that's great. And your parents?"

I shake my head. "It's just my brothers and me now."

"I see." She looks deep in thought, and I wonder what she could be thinking.

"Have you decided?" I gesture to the menu she's still holding.

"Not yet. What about you, since you've been here before, what do you recommend?"

I give the steaks and seafood listed barely a passing glance. "All of their pasta is homemade."

"Those are my two favorite words."

"Then we should indulge."

She grins, closing her menu. "Pasta, it is."

We share a *caprese* salad and enjoy it with generous chunks of bread dipped in the most delicious olive oil.

"This is incredible," Alessandra says, her voice low.

The restaurant's soft lighting and the flickering candle on our table give everything a romantic glow, and so while it should feel too intimate for a first date, it's actually perfect.

"I'm glad you said yes."

Her gaze is on mine again. "Me, too."

Our food is delivered to the table, two large porcelain bowls heaped with the most delicious-looking pasta. A simple, classic spaghetti Bolognese for her, and penne with olive oil and grilled shrimp for me.

The expression on Alessandra's face is pure delight as she digs in and tastes her first bite of pasta. "Oh, dear God," she says on a moan.

Watching her eat is more enjoyable than partaking myself, and I take a sip from my glass, appreciating the view.

"To your liking?"

She nods enthusiastically, wiping the corner of her mouth with her white cloth napkin. "Amazing."

"*Vuoi venire a casa mia per mangiare pene?*" I ask.

Alessandra's eyes widen, and she pauses with her wineglass halfway to her lips, looking alarmed. "*Penne* is pasta. *Pene* is something else entirely," she says, her tone hushed.

I push my plate toward her. "I was trying to ask if you wanted a bite of my pasta."

Her mouth curves into a grin. "You asked me if I wanted to eat your dick."

"For fuck's sake." I set my fork down and shake my head. "I'm sorry. I meant to save that question for after dessert."

This earns me another laugh. It's honest and raw, and I love the sound of it already.

"Probably a good idea," she says with a chuckle.

"Call me old fashioned, but tiramisu first, and then dick-eating."

Alessandra laughs again before taking me up on my offer and spearing a forkful of penne pasta from my bowl.

It's strange. The conversation flows as easily as the wine. While we should have nothing in common—her, a young twenty-something fresh out of college; and me, a late-thirties CEO who's grown a little jaded on the world—yet here we are, laughing and smiling and having an amazing time.

As the evening rolls on, I find myself more and more enamored with her. And as nice as it is to spend time with her, I already know how the evening will end. I'm a gentleman, and I'm not the type to sleep with a woman on the first date.

In my younger years, I was no stranger to one-night stands, but this is different. Alessandra isn't some random girl I've met at a bar who's looking for a quick roll between the sheets. And if I'm being honest, there's something I like about this slow seduction—the back and forth of getting to know each other, the flirting. I know it will make it that much more intense when we do finally come together.

We finish dinner, lingering over wine. I'm not quite ready for the night to end, and I can't help but sense Alessandra feels the same.

"Dessert?" I ask.

"Next time," she says, and I can't help but watch the

way her lips move. I'm equally thrilled about the possibility of there being a next time as I am about watching her eat dessert from my spoon.

After paying the check and adding a generous tip, I usher Alessandra to the door and out to where the waiting cab is that I've called. It's too late for her to take public transportation alone. We stop on the curb together, huddled close.

"I had a wonderful time," I say, watching her eyes as she tilts her face up to mine.

"Me, too," she murmurs, her tongue coming out to wet her bottom lip.

Blood surges south, and the desire to take her home nearly overwhelms me. Instead, I place my hand on the back of her neck and guide her mouth to mine.

The moment our lips meet, it's fucking electric. Our lips move perfectly in sync together, and the second her mouth parts, my tongue sweeps against hers, tasting sweet wine and her. It takes every ounce of self-control I have to pull away, and when I do, the dreamy half-lidded look on her face is everything.

I take a deep breath, fighting to compose myself and the erection I can feel nudging the front of my pants. "Good night, Alessandra."

"Good night, Quinn."

I open the car door and tuck her inside, and when she pulls away, I'm filled with a sense of buoyancy and hope that I haven't felt in a long time.

Chapter Three

Alessandra

Saturday mornings are reserved for sleeping as late as my body will let me, a desperate attempt to make up for all the REM cycles I miss out on by waking up at sunrise to play "Mom" for ten hours a day during the week.

Most weekends, I don't even bother getting out of my pajamas, spending lazy days sprawled across my bedroom floor, scrolling through travel blogs on my laptop, and dog-earing pages in any one of the dozens of Italian travel guides I have stacked next to the bed. Sure, I love the nightlife in Boston, but fifty hours a week of chasing the little devils I look after warrants a bit of time to recharge and plan my Italian adventure. Well, not to be confused with the Italian adventure that kissed the living daylights out of me last night.

But this Saturday isn't a day for flipping through travel guides. Since I sacrificed my usual routine of enjoying wine and reality TV with Deanna on Friday for an evening out with one of the richest men in Boston, I promised Deanna a full day of thrift shopping to make up for it.

We're doing our best to squeeze out every last minute of best-friend time before I board the plane. I've never been in a long-distance relationship, but I get the feeling that being an ocean away from Deanna will be similarly taxing. She and I haven't spent more than a week at a time apart since we met at a foreign-language-department barbecue our freshman year of college. I was there to meet other students in the department, and she was there to snag a free burger.

This is pretty typical of our dynamic. Deanna is spontaneous and bold, the perfect college bestie who dragged me to parties and karaoke nights when I had spent one-too-many weekends with my nose contentedly buried in the pages of Plato or Seneca. She brings out the wilder side of me, the side that does things like buy a one-way ticket to Italy or, apparently, go on a date with a handsome billionaire who was born in a decade that I only know as a theme for a fraternity party.

Deanna's signature three honks announce her arrival in my driveway as I'm brushing my teeth, still in my pajamas.

Shit. Piling my hair into a messy bun, I throw on leggings and a cozy tee that I stole from her and I'm out the door, not even caring I'm fresh-faced without makeup. Deanna isn't someone I have to work to impress. She loves me just as I am. It's pretty much amazing.

"Good morning, sunshine!"

I climb into the passenger seat of her tiny red two-seater and am greeted with some unrecognizable electronic song shaking the whole car. Deanna's short blonde hair is pushed back in a headband and a gray sweater drapes over her frame, instantly making me feel better about my lazy getup. She sips at her coffee, handing me a matching to-go cup. I take a sip—skim chai latte, my absolute favorite. Can I just take this girl to Italy with me? She's like the wife I need in my life.

As she shifts the car into reverse, Deanna turns down the music enough that we can talk over it without yelling. "So, spill. How was dinner with the Italian stallion?"

I nearly spit chai latte all over the dashboard. "Oh, my God, I'm not telling you *anything* if you call him that."

"Yeah, right." Deanna rolls her eyes, chuckling.

We haven't spared each other a single detail of our romantic encounters in all four years of our friendship. She would never let me start now, even if there is something about Quinn that makes me want to keep him all to myself.

"It was great. Like, really great. I'd never been to a restaurant where the prices are so high that they don't even list them."

Deanna rolls her eyes. "A little less menu, a little more men. Skip to the good stuff, please."

I half smile and take a swig of my chai latte, mentally fast-forwarding through an evening of trying to focus on Quinn's beautiful broken Italian while wishing I was the rim of the wineglass between his lips. I give Deanna what she wants to hear.

"He's smart, and funny and sweet. Honestly, I have no idea how he's still single."

"Yeah, that is sort of weird." She's watching the road, but I don't miss the way her eyes narrow slightly as she thinks it over.

"But it was great talking to someone so intelligent

and charming." Bantering with him in Italian still brings a smile to my face.

Deanna nods, listening.

"And he's an amazing kisser."

Slamming the heels of her hands excitedly on the wheel, Deanna accidentally honks her horn a few times. The guy in the minivan at the stoplight next to us looks over, totally confused, but Deanna doesn't seem to care. As soon as the light turns green, she makes a hard-left turn into the parking lot of our favorite thrift store, letting out an excited squeal.

"Damn, Aly. Making out with a billionaire. I'm so proud. And slightly jealous."

She parks the car and lets the song finish as we down the rest of our coffees. I put my story on pause for the sake of caffeine. Priorities.

The store is empty other than the woman behind the counter, who seems pretty wrapped up in her sudoku puzzle, so I don't even bother keeping my voice down as I recount the details of my evening. As we thumb through racks of vintage dresses and faux-leather jackets, I give her the full play-by-play, including every detail from the way Quinn's chocolate-brown eyes traced my hips when I walked into the restaurant, to the taste of pinot noir on his lower lip. A hot shiver races along my skin at the memory of our kiss. I'd never been kissed like that, so sure and demanding. He knew exactly what he was doing— commanding his body, and in turn, mine.

As I talk, I realize it's awfully refreshing to tell a story of an encounter with a guy that doesn't include an unsolicited dick pic or an impressive beer-pong performance.

"I could get used to this older-man thing pretty damn quickly," I admit, feeling the blood rushing to my cheeks as I say it. I can't believe I'm so smitten already.

"Like, three weeks quickly?" Deanna tosses a dress at me. It's black and lacy and ultra-short, erring on the side of lingerie.

"I sort of maybe didn't mention the moving-to-Italy thing last night," I confess, holding the dress up to me. "It didn't really come up."

"Okay, sure, nowhere in your dinner conversation that was half-spoken in Italian did it come up that you're moving to Italy. Sounds legit. Go try that on; you'd look hot in it."

Deanna follows me into the fitting room—we're way beyond the point of personal boundaries. I throw my clothes in a pile in the corner and step into the dress, which fits better than a glove, more like a second skin. She zips me in and lets out a wolf whistle as we both get a look at my reflection in the mirror. It's tight in the best kind of way, the stretchy material clinging to my hips and ass, and the black lace frames the perfect amount of cleavage.

"All I'm saying is if I were him and my Italian tutor showed up looking like that, I'd double up on lessons," Deanna says with a wink.

I imagine myself slipping this on before my next meeting with Quinn, almost certain he would slip it off me before the lesson even started. I do only have three weeks, after all.

Chapter Four

Quinn

The next week starts off with a bang, all because of a particularly high-powered client who can't be bothered to settle his bill.

My brothers and I try to avoid doing business with men like him who think that their status is payment enough. Over the years, we've become more selective when it comes to our clients, precisely for reasons like this. But even despite our best efforts to weed out the stingy pricks, every once in a while one of them worms his way into our system. In those cases, we're forced to track him down and remind him that the pretty little thing on his arm is only there because he's paying her, and by paying her, I mean paying us.

When I suggest that we stay late one night to put an end to this issue, the two of them exchange a look.

"Can't," Cooper says, rubbing the back of his neck. "Corinne's making lasagna tonight. It's one of our traditions."

I groan and roll my eyes before turning to Gavin. "What's your excuse?"

"No mushy traditions." Gavin shrugs. "I just want to fuck my wife, and she's less in the mood when I get home late."

I shake my head. "Fine. Let's take a problem that could be solved in one night and drag it out for the rest of the week. Great plan, douchebags."

But not even my sarcasm can pop the bubble of happiness both my brothers are in because of their marriages. Those little fuckers. Gavin and Emma are coming up on their second anniversary, and Cooper and Corinne are newlyweds, but things have changed so much already.

Cooper, Gavin, and I spend the next few days playing phone tag and negotiating with the client. In the old days, we would have been able to knock it all out in one night, but Cooper and Gavin are both so happily married, they choose to drag the process out a few days just so they can go home to their wives each night at a decent time and revel in their wedded bliss.

I'm happy for the assholes, but marriage has definitely made them soft.

• • •

By Thursday, I realize that the sting of jealousy I feel toward my brothers has everything to do with Alessandra. We've only been on a single date, but I can already tell there's something different about her.

Hell, the fact that we went on a date at all is evidence enough that she's special. I've had plenty of experience with women, but those escapades rarely ever made it out of the bedroom. It's not that I don't want to do those same things to Alessandra—you can't imagine the things I've fantasized about doing to her—but no matter how powerful my desire is for her, I can't silence the small voice in the back of my head telling me I'm in serious danger of falling.

That's why I'm determined to take it slow with this girl. Or, at least, slower than I would normally take it.

Sitting at my desk, I hear a gentle knock on my office door. Six p.m. on the dot, right on time. I stand up to open the door, but I'm immediately stopped by a strange feeling in my stomach.

Were those butterflies? Jesus, Quinn, get your shit together.

I take a deep breath and stretch out my neck. For as excited as I am to spend more time with Alessandra, I'm not too pleased with the effect she's having on me.

When I open the door to my office, it takes everything in me not to immediately sweep her into my arms and place a kiss on her lips. She's intoxicating. Her dark hair is piled loosely on top of her head, and a few stray curls perfectly frame her face. She looks up at me with cautious-yet-playful eyes, obviously waiting for me to invite her in.

"*Benevenuto.*" I smile, stepping aside and ushering her in.

As Alessandra walks past me, I can't help but take in every inch of her nubile body, the way her perfect ass fills out her dark blue jeans. She even smells amazing, somewhat floral and sweet. She sets her bag in one of the chairs by my desk and stands by the windows, just like she did the first day she came here.

I close the door behind me and take a moment before joining her. As I take in the full sight of her, my cock twitching in approval, I rack my brain for the small bit of Italian I've been practicing all week for this very moment.

"*Tu mi toglie il fiato*," I say, closing the distance between us. *You take my breath away.*

Alessandra turns and smiles at me, her eyes wide and playful. "*Grazie mille*," she replies, sizing me up. "You've been practicing."

"You make me want to practice," I say, my voice low and serious.

The smile fades from her face and she arches a single perfect brow. "Do I make you want to do anything else?" she asks, taking a step closer so our faces are only inches apart.

Holy fuck.

Without speaking, I wrap her slender frame in my arms, crushing my mouth against hers in a hungry, searching kiss. After a moment's hesitation, Alessandra responds by pressing her hips into me and moving her tongue in rhythm with mine. It's beyond perfect.

We continue kissing, our hands moving over each

other's bodies, until Alessandra suddenly pulls back and looks at me with wide, concerned eyes.

"Should we be kissing in your office?" she asks, looking nervously over her shoulder. "I just realized I know nothing about office etiquette, and I really don't like the idea of you getting in trouble because I'm too horny to keep my tongue in my own mouth while I tutor you." As soon as the words leave her mouth, she grimaces, obviously embarrassed by what she just said.

I chuckle softly, trying not to make her feel any worse, even though she has no reason to be embarrassed. She has no idea how adorable she is. Or how fucking sexy it is to hear the word *horny* come out of her mouth.

I pull her back into me and place a hand on her cheek. "Alessandra," I whisper, running my thumb over her jaw, "you're forgetting one very important thing. I'm the boss around here. You'd have to do many worse things with your tongue for either of us to get in trouble."

She smiles, looking down for a moment before her gaze flits back to mine. When we lock eyes, I imagine all the things she could do with her tongue. My cock twitches again, and by the way she arches her brow, this time

Alessandra can feel it. She wraps her arms even tighter around me, pressing her body more purposefully against my bulge. Within moments, her lips are moving feverishly against mine, soft moans escaping from her lips as I move my thigh between her legs.

Suddenly, we're interrupted by Alyssa's bright and chipper voice over the intercom. "Quinn, your brother is here to see you." She may be the world's most efficient assistant, but her timing is horrendous.

Alessandra pulls away from me, her eyes wide and embarrassed. "Oh, my God," she mutters quietly under her breath. She pulls a compact out of her purse and groans as she examines the state of her hair. "We're so busted."

"Everything's fine. We're not doing anything wrong," I say, though to be honest, I find her little freak-out adorable.

"Yeah? Tell that to your tie. And you might want to wipe the lipstick off your face before letting your brother in."

So full of life. So fucking sexy.

As Alessandra continues fixing her hair, I straighten my tie and walk to the door, while I surreptitiously run the back of my hand over my mouth in case Alessandra wasn't just teasing me about the lipstick.

I open the door to find Cooper standing there, a bemused smile spreading across his face.

"Yes?" I say, deliberately blocking the doorway. I haven't told my brothers about my new Italian tutor, and while I'm by no means ashamed of Alessandra, I'm more than a little aware of our age difference. I don't want to put unnecessary pressure on her by introducing her to my family.

"Have a minute? I wanted to run the final numbers on this jackass so we can tuck his file away for good," Cooper says, trying to walk around me into my office.

"Now's not a good time. I'm in the middle of an Italian lesson."

"Sal's here? How's he doing? God, I haven't seen that guy in forever," Cooper says, peeking around me.

I love my brother, but he can be a nosy little fucker sometimes.

"Not Sal," Alessandra says from behind me, her voice light and playful.

Cooper raises his eyebrows. Without saying a word, he pushes past me into my office.

"I'm Alessandra. It's nice to meet you," she says, holding out her hand to him.

"*Piacere di conoscerti*," Cooper says, shaking her hand and bowing slightly.

I know he only said *nice to meet you*, but the playful glint in his eye rubs me the wrong way.

"You Kingsley brothers must have been keeping Sal busy." Alessandra chuckles, her eyes bright and cheery.

After seeing how nervous she was to be caught in the middle of making out, I'm in awe of how quickly she pulled herself together. Brilliant, beautiful, and good under pressure? This woman is making it nearly impossible not to fall for her.

Cooper laughs and shakes his head. "I had a particularly memorable vacation in Italy years ago."

Alessandra smiles, and Cooper gives me a

questioning look.

"I'll get out of your hair. See you at dinner this Sunday," he says, turning and walking to the door. Before leaving, he stops and looks back at Alessandra. "Will you be there? Sal never could make it, but it's nice getting to know the people who are regularly coming in and out of our building."

Alessandra looks at me, her eyes wide and curious. "Oh, I don't think so," she says, but I cut her off.

"No, that's a great idea. You should come." I give her my most reassuring smile.

Cooper nods, tells us he'll see us Sunday, and promptly exits the room, leaving Alessandra and me to discuss what just happened.

"Quinn, if it's too complicated to have me there, I really don't have to come." She plops herself down in one of the chairs in front of my desk and rakes her fingers through her hair.

"I think it's a great idea," I say, sitting in the chair next to her. "I understand if it feels like a lot, but I like spending time with you, and I want to do more of that."

Alessandra nods, though she still looks unsure. "Okay. I'd love to."

"Good. It's settled." I shift in my seat, so painfully aware of her that for the first time, I realize that actually concentrating on learning a foreign language is going to be difficult. "*Iniziamo?*" I ask. *Shall we begin?*

Alessandra nods, and we launch into a friendly conversation that I barely manage to keep clean.

I need to up my game at flirtatious Italian phrases.

By the time our hour is up, Alessandra rises to her feet, placing the strap of her purse high on her slender shoulder, and a rock settles in the pit of my stomach.

"What are you doing Saturday?" I blurt. "There's an art exhibit featuring classic Italian artists at the museum. Want to meet for coffee and go check it out? Late morning, maybe? We could breakfast if you like."

I smile and imagine the two of us huddled together at a small café table, laughing over my Italian accent. It's a cheesy daydream, I know, but I can't deny how much I've enjoyed this gorgeous woman's presence in my life.

Alessandra smiles softly at me, but I note a touch of

hesitation as she speaks. "That sounds lovely, Quinn," she says, tucking her hair behind her ear. "But there's something I need to tell you."

I nod and wait for her to continue, bracing myself for another one of her adorable feisty quips.

"I'm leaving for Italy in a few weeks. It's a one-way ticket. . .. I'm moving there, giving up my job as a nanny to start a new life. I've enjoyed spending time with you— truly, I have—I just think it's important that I'm honest with you. This thing we have, it can't develop into something more. I've wanted to move to Italy for so long, and now that it's happening, I can't let anything or anyone keep me from fulfilling that dream."

Fuck. Her words strike right through me, so hard that I swear I actually flinch.

Though my mind is reeling, I hold myself together. After taking a deep breath, I lift her chin and look deeply into her soft brown eyes, stroking her cheek with my thumb. "All the more reason to enjoy your company now while I still have you stateside."

Alessandra smiles, her eyes crinkling in the corners.

"Pick me up at ten Saturday morning?"

"Ten, it is."

I draw her face to mine and place a gentle kiss on her lips before she gathers her things to leave.

As Alessandra walks out of my office, my mind is racing with a thousand thoughts about what's happening, what I will do, and how I should feel. Though I don't know how to move forward with this woman who blows my mind a little more every time I see her, one thought rings loud and clear above the rest.

I'd better make the next few weeks worth it.

Chapter Five

Alessandra

I wake up Saturday morning feeling panicked and excited at the same time.

As I hop in the shower and wash my hair, my thoughts return to my evening with Quinn. . .for about the thirty-fifth time in the two days since then. The way he took me in his arms and kissed me with such passion, and then we traded flirty comments in Italian. . .it was all so unbelievably sexy. I can already tell I'll have a hard time keeping my cool on this date.

After stepping out of the shower, I dry off and slip into the fuzzy purple bathrobe my mom bought me last Christmas, and wrap my long, dark hair up in my towel.

What does one wear on a day date? And a classy day date, at that. Something about the sound of an Italian artists' exhibit tells me that Quinn will make sure our breakfast outing is fancy, too. I love going out for breakfast, and thinking about the kind of breakfast food waiting for me on this date makes my stomach growl.

After a lot of indecisiveness, I finally settle on a pale blue wrap dress and strappy tan sandals. The dress makes me feel sexy by hinting at just the right amount of cleavage, while the mid-calf hemline makes me feel sophisticated enough to be worthy of admiring centuries-old works of art.

I throw my mostly dry hair into a loose side braid, swipe on a couple coats of mascara, and finish applying a layer of pinkish nude lipstick just as I hear a knock on my door. Grabbing my purse, I take one last look at myself in the mirror, adjust a stray bra strap, and hurry to the front door to greet Quinn.

When I open the door, for a moment I forget how to breathe.

Quinn Kingsley will be the death of me.

I've only ever seen him in a suit, and if that sight was hard to handle, Saturday-morning-casual Quinn is simply too much. Dressed in dark-wash jeans and a tan cashmere sweater that perfectly outlines his chiseled chest and shoulders, he stands there smiling at me, his massive frame taking up my entire doorway. A pair of sunglasses hang on his collar, and just the faintest bit of scruff perfectly defines his jaw.

Jesus, his sex appeal is off the charts today.

"*Buongiorno, bellissima signora,*" he murmurs, leaning down to kiss me on the cheek. *Good morning, beautiful lady.*

All right, that's just not fair.

"*Buongiorno, signore,*" I reply, shyly tucking my hair behind my ear. Part of me wishes I could think of something sexier to say, but honestly, it's impressive I'm able to get any words out, let alone Italian ones.

When we arrive at his car, Quinn opens the door for me, shutting it gently after I swing my legs inside. On the drive to the café, we continue chatting in Italian, mostly about what we want to eat for breakfast.

The whole time we're talking, I can't help but watch the way he smiles a little every time he speaks, proud of the Italian sentences he's able to string together. For as mature and experienced as Quinn clearly is, I love seeing little glimpses of the youth still in him. Like how he squints his eyes slightly when he's trying to think of the right word, or the look he gives me just before kissing me...

"Alessandra?" Quinn's voice breaks through my thoughts, just in time to stop me from entering a full-blown fantasy.

"Sorry," I say, shaking my head. "I was thinking about conjugations."

He smiles and reaches over to take my hand in his. "What's it like to have such a big brain?" he murmurs, raising a playful eyebrow. "I can only imagine what's going on in there."

My stomach drops at his touch, and I feel a familiar tingle between my legs.

Oh, you have no idea.

• • •

After finishing our coffee and scones at the café, Quinn and I walk through the exhibit at the museum. The paintings are breathtaking. I took a couple of art history classes in college, so as I stand in front of some of the paintings we talked about in class, I can hear my professors' voices explaining the intricacies of the brushstrokes and the significance of the time periods when the pieces were painted.

Quinn, as usual, is perfect throughout the exhibit. I was worried that he might be the kind of date to stay right by my side the entire time, to insist on making comments on the art every five seconds. I'm used to stupid college boys who took me to museums because they thought it would make them look smart, only to talk the entire time and only really look at one or two paintings.

But like every other time I prepared for Quinn to disappoint me, he reminds me that he is, without a doubt, the most mature, sophisticated man I've ever dated. He held my hand while we wandered together, listening as spoke about the paintings I'd studied in school. He's sweet, and thoughtful, and smart. In short, he's perfect. And me? I'm determined to match him in sophistication and maturity.

As we near the end of the exhibit, Quinn returns to my side, placing his hand on my lower back to guide me to the exit. We walk to the car, my hand on his arm once again, discussing our favorite paintings. He teases me a little about how excited I am that they have a Botticelli, but I can tell from the crinkles in the corners of his eyes that he really is just teasing, and that part of him is genuinely impressed.

"Hungry?" he asks, opening my car door for me once again.

"Starving," I reply as I climb into my seat. That scone from earlier was good, but it was nowhere near enough to hold me over.

"There's a farmers' market on the way to my place. What do you say we swing by there to pick up some fruit and cheese, maybe some good bread, and make ourselves a Mediterranean lunch?"

I nod enthusiastically, shifting in my seat as my stomach grumbles at the thought of our meal. And at the idea of seeing where he lives.

At the farmers' market, Quinn leads me deftly through the stands, pointing out which vendors have the best bread, the most perfectly aged cheese, the freshest fruit. It's clear he frequents this market often, and I swoon a little at the thought of Quinn wandering here alone on the weekends. Once again, how in the fresh hell is he still single?

Everything feels so perfect when I'm with him. It's been the kind of day my friends and I used to dream about in college, where the smart, sexy, sophisticated man orders all the right food, asks all the right questions, and listens to what you have to say with *genuine interest*.

The more time I spend with Quinn, there's this little niggling thought forming in the recesses of my mind, and it's telling me that I'm less excited about my move to Italy. Which scares me because that one-way ticket is what I've been dreaming about my entire life.

Back at his place, Quinn makes our items from the farmers' market into a beautiful charcuterie plate with such ease, I'm starting to worry that he's almost too sophisticated. What could he possibly see in a twenty-two-year-old like me—who can barely make mac and cheese—let alone artfully assemble hors d'oeuvres?

"*Bravo*," I murmur as Quinn places the platter on the table in front of me.

"*Grazie*." He smiles, popping a grape into his mouth, my eyes watching his every move.

How does he make eating fruit look so sexy?

I tear off a piece of the Italian bread, place a small slice of Parmigiano Reggiano on top, and take a bite of the combination, closing my eyes and moaning softly as the cheese hits my tongue. I thought I knew what good cheese tastes like, but this? This is better than anything I've ever had in my mouth before.

When I open my eyes, I look up to see Quinn staring at me, one eyebrow raised.

"What can I do to make you make that sound again?" he asks, his voice low and gravelly.

Composing myself, I smile at him, that same familiar tingle between my legs. "For starters," I murmur, placing my elbows on the table and leaning forward so Quinn can steal a glance down the front of my dress, "you could give me another piece of that cheese."

His gaze wanders lazily over my body, moving from my eyes to my chest and then back up to my face. Watching him take in the sight of me makes me feel like my skin is on fire, and I relish the slow anticipation of what comes next.

Taking a slice of cheese between his thumb and index finger, Quinn raises it to my mouth, looking at me expectantly. We lock eyes and I open my mouth, the tingle between my thighs quickly becoming an ache. He places the cheese on my tongue and I moan again, louder and more satisfied than before. If this is a game of seduction, I'm determined to win.

I chew slowly, keeping my eyes trained on Quinn's. He watches me with a fire in his eyes I've never seen before. I raise an eyebrow, daring him to make the first move.

"Fuck it," he growls, abruptly standing and pulling my body up against his. All at once, he crushes his mouth against mine, his hands moving firmly over my hips.

Rising to my tiptoes, I respond to his kiss, wrapping my arms around his broad shoulders. As our kiss deepens, he picks me up, placing my legs on either side of his hips as he marches us over to his couch, his lips never leaving mine. Gently, he lays me on the couch, pausing to look me over once more before descending over top of me, his mouth moving to my neck, where he coaxes small moans from me as his tongue moves over my skin.

With one arm supporting his body weight, Quinn lets his other hand roam freely, gently massaging my breast before finding the tie of my dress and slowly pulling it undone. I can't believe how patient he's being, each movement purposeful and unhurried. I'm used to the kind of guys who barely wait two seconds before shoving my head down to their lap. But from this position, I can't even reach to unfasten Quinn's jeans, and he doesn't seem to care at all.

God, it's gonna be hard to leave this man behind.

As the thought passes through my mind, Quinn slips his hand inside my dress, running his fingers over my stomach and down between my legs, pausing just before my soaking-wet panties. For a moment, he stops kissing my neck, raising his head to look me in the eye.

"Is this okay??" His voice is raw and husky, and the sound of it sends a chill racing through me.

"Si."

He dips his fingers under the elastic of my panties and between my swollen lips. I gasp as he massages my clit with small, circular motions, and he places his mouth on mine again, kissing away my increasing moans.

He continues moving his fingers, bringing me to the brink of orgasm before stopping suddenly, moving his mouth to my breast and rolling my nipple between his lips.

"Why'd—you—stop?" I ask between breaths, feeling needier than I have in my entire life.

"Patience," he growls, softly nibbling on my fully hardened nipple. "It's called edging."

I'm about to speak again when he slowly thrusts his fingers inside me, pumping quickly while running his thumb over my sensitive center. Within moments, the most powerful orgasm I've ever had in my life washes over me, and I swear I almost black out. As my body slowly stops its spasms, Quinn holds me even closer, placing tender kisses onto my neck and my lips. Almost like he enjoyed my orgasm as much as I did.

Once I regain my ability to breathe, I kiss him back, pushing him up into a sitting position and swinging my leg around to straddle him. We continue kissing, and I move my mouth to his neck, sucking and nibbling before reaching down to unbutton his jeans, and whisper, "Should we move to your bedroom?" I can feel his stiff erection under my hands, and based on how amazing he is with his fingers, I can only imagine the kinds of things he knows how to do with his cock.

Quinn pauses, pulling his face away and placing his

hands on top of mine. "I was hoping to take you on a proper date before we did that," he says, sighing a little at his own resolve.

"I'd hardly call what we just did taking it slow." I chuckle, experimentally touching the hard ridge through his jeans.

He groans and lifts me off him, placing me gently by his side. "I guess I'm just old-fashioned, but I'd like to take you out first. And not on a day date that started with coffee. I'm talking a nice dinner, dressed up. . .the works."

That's unexpected.

I sigh and place my hand against his cheek. "You're very sweet," I say, kissing him softly. "I, uh, guess I'll see you tomorrow, then. You're cooking, right?" I stand and begin gathering my things.

"Yes, ma'am," Quinn replies, standing to join me.

"Anything I can bring?"

"Nothing but your presence. And maybe your patience."

"Oh. Is this something I need to prepare for?" I ask,

my stomach churning.

Are his brothers assholes? Do they hate me? Am I causing a scandal in the Kingsley family? Suddenly, I'm nervous about this family dinner.

"No, no. Well, maybe. Actually, no, it'll be fine," Quinn says, obviously unsure how to respond.

"Oh, great, now that you've removed all doubt, I feel better."

Quinn chuckles and pulls me into his arms. "My brothers will love you. As will their wives. It's only that. . .well, sometimes when all three of us get together, it can be a lot."

"A lot in what way?" I'm curious now and doing my best not to panic.

"Well. . .Gavin is the broody one, though his wife, Emma, has significantly lightened him up. If it feels like he's being cold to you, don't take it personally. That's just how he is."

I nod, making mental notes. "What about Cooper?"

"Cooper is the family romantic. He and Gavin have a

bit of a choppy history, but they're better now. Cooper married Corinne last year, who is the sweetest little thing you'll ever meet. They're still in their honeymoon phase, so try not to let their sappiness annoy you."

I nod again, remembering Cooper's playful grin when we met in Quinn's office. Broody, romantic, sappy. . .there's a lot to remember, but I'm fairly confident I can successfully navigate their family dynamic.

I place a final kiss on Quinn's lips before heading to the door. "Thank you for today—the museum, the lunch."

He nods once and presses a warm kiss to my palm. "See you tomorrow, *bella*."

On the way home, my mind is still reeling from the perfect date we had. . .as well as the perfect ending. Looking back, to every date with every man who has shared my bed, there's honestly no comparison to Quinn. There's never been a man before him who has pleasured me and didn't expect quid pro quo. Even though I wanted to go farther with him, I can't help but smile at his old-fashioned ways which I find a huge turn-on. It's ramping up my anticipation of our first time together and it's almost more than I can handle right now. I also have to keep reminding myself that I'm leaving in three weeks…three short weeks. I need a distraction, something that's going to take my mind off of the predicament I find myself in with Quinn.

I spend the rest of the day cleaning my apartment and picking out an outfit for dinner the next night. If dressing for a day date was tricky, dressing for a Sunday family dinner is even trickier.

As I rifle through my closet, doing my best to find an outfit that says *I'm not some twenty-two-year-old bimbo dating your brother for his money*, I can't ignore the concern I have over meeting his brothers…and for the possibility that I'm falling a little head over heels for this man, whether I want to or not.

Chapter Six

Quinn

Turning on the oven light, I lean over and squint through the glass door to check on the tenderloin. I know it isn't done, but I need an excuse to ignore my brothers for a moment, who won't stop asking me about the twenty-two-year-old tutor joining us for dinner this evening.

"Needs another ten to fifteen," I say gruffly as I stand up. "Alessandra should be here any minute, so I suppose I should get started on the wedges."

I make my way to the fridge, continuing to ignore my brothers' slightly judgmental stares, and pull out a couple of heads of iceberg lettuce to begin the process of preparing our first course.

"You can't dodge our questions forever, you know," Cooper says, a stupid grin lifting the corners of his mouth.

When I don't respond, he nudges Gavin, who takes a long sip of his wine before saying, "Look, we're glad you've finally started dating after thirteen years of 'I'm too busy for that shit', but we're worried that you've fallen into an 'I'm too old for this shit' situation."

I roll my eyes. "Alessandra is unlike any other woman I've met. If you guys would just give her a chance tonight, I promise, all this will make sense."

"Of course she's unlike any other woman you've met. She was still in diapers when you got your first hard-on." Gavin scoffs, downing the rest of his glass.

"I can't believe you, of all people, are giving me a hard time for dating a younger woman. It's not like you've never been there before," I say, slicing the last wedge of lettuce with gusto.

Gavin's eyes narrow. "And look how well that ended."

I know I'll regret dredging up his past like that later, but I'm quickly growing tired of my brothers' judgment. Especially since they've both had colorful romantic pasts of their own.

"We're just worried about you, that's all," Cooper says, placing a hand on my shoulder.

Shrugging his hand off me, I plate the wedges, then

drizzle the lettuce with my homemade dressing and sprinkle crumbled bacon on top. "I don't need you to worry. I need you to give Alessandra a chance."

Just as I finish talking, Emma and Corinne enter the kitchen, partly to join our conversation, but mostly to refill their glasses of rosé.

"Yes, when will Alessandra be arriving?" Emma asks, arching a perfectly plucked brow at me. "When Gavin told me you were dating, I couldn't wait to meet the lucky girl." As she speaks, she moves to stand next to Gavin, placing her hand in the center of his back.

I watch as Corinne instinctively does the same thing, standing next to Cooper and looping her arm around his. I'm happy for my brothers, but it's becoming uncomfortable being the only unmarried Kingsley brother.

Before I can answer Emma, the doorbell rings and a wave of relief washes over me. It's easy for my brothers to ask their judgmental questions, but I know they're socially competent enough to be cordial in Alessandra's presence, whether they approve of our relationship or not.

But, dammit, I just want them to give her a chance.

As I walk to the front door, I turn and give Gavin and Cooper one last *behave yourselves* look, to which they both shrug and furrow their brows.

I open the door to find Alessandra standing there, a bottle of wine in one hand and an olive tray in the other. Despite the worried look on her face, she looks as gorgeous as ever, her long, dark hair swept into a side braid, perfectly complementing the off-the-shoulder top she paired with jeans that hug her curves in all the right places.

As I stand there, taking her in, a whispered *bellissima* crosses my lips without my even thinking about it.

For a moment, Alessandra's face softens, and she quickly steps toward me to plant a grateful kiss on my lips. If it weren't for the wine and the olive tray in her hands, I would fully embrace her, but I don't want to stress her out even more.

As we part, she scurries into the entryway behind me, and before walking into the kitchen, turns and begins talking faster than I've ever heard her talk before.

"I know you told me not to bring anything, but my

mom always said you should never walk into a party empty-handed, and I was worried that if I didn't bring something, your brothers would think I was just another asshole millennial, so I don't know what you're making tonight, but I hope it goes with wine and olives. Is the braid okay? Am I dressed nice enough? I didn't want to overdo it, but I also wanted to communicate that I'm respectful of the family Sunday dinner tradition—"

Before she can continue, I cut her off by leaning in and placing another kiss on her lips. For a moment, Alessandra freezes, obviously surprised by the gesture. But within seconds, she softens again, parting her lips and running her tongue gently around mine.

Suddenly, she breaks away, her eyes frantic. "My lipstick! We can't walk in there with lipstick all over our faces!" She begins pacing, searching the walls of my home for a mirror. "You're lucky I decided to go with a nude. If I'd worn the darker color, we'd both be toast."

I chuckle and run the back of my hand over my mouth to wipe off any traces of lipstick.

Alessandra smiles and uses her thumb to rub a bit of lipstick off my upper lip. "Am I good?" she asks, turning her face from side to side.

"Perfect," I say, smiling broadly at her. "They're going to love you. Especially Emma and Corinne—they do love a good red."

She smiles and follows me into the kitchen, where both Cooper and Gavin stand to greet her. They each shake Alessandra's hand and exchange pleasantries before returning to their seats at the bar of the island, at which point Emma and Corinne descend upon her. They shower Alessandra with praises and questions about her hair, her clothes, and her choice of wine, greeting her with the kind of excitement I've only ever seen occur between women.

It's clear to me in this moment that my sisters-in-law have decided together to make every effort possible to make Alessandra feel comfortable, regardless of their husbands' reservations about her. I've never been more grateful for their taste in women, even if my two brothers weren't as sweet and as welcoming as their wives.

Once the welcoming committee dies down, I pour Alessandra a glass of wine, and she takes it from me so quickly, I'm almost surprised when she doesn't drain it. For as nervous as I know she is, Alessandra is handling the situation like a champ, and I make a note to myself to remember to tell her so later.

"So, Alessandra," Cooper says, swirling the wine in his glass. "Quinn's told us you've just graduated with a degree in. . .Italian?"

"Classics," she says, smiling and nodding her head as she corrects him. "But yes, I studied Italian, as well."

"And what do classics majors do after college?" Gavin asks. I'm not sure, but it seems to me that his sharp gaze is somehow more piercing than usual.

Alessandra chuckles, tucking her hair behind her ear before answering. "I've been a nanny since I graduated, along with the tutoring. It doesn't sound like a lot, but it's been enough to get by." She pauses, her gaze flitting nervously to me before settling back on Gavin. "I've been saving up, actually, because I'm moving to Italy in a few weeks to teach. That's been my dream for years, and I'm finally in a position to make it happen."

While Emma and Corinne respond with the appropriate level of excitement to Alessandra's news about Italy, I can't ignore the concern on my brothers' faces. Gavin and Cooper exchange hesitant looks with each other, then look at me with their brows raised.

Their expressions say it all. We don't always get along, but my brothers and I are still pretty in sync. They're worried about me. And if I'm being honest with myself, hearing Alessandra talk about leaving the country again, even after the time we've been spending together, sends pangs of worry and sadness coursing through me.

Before Gavin or Cooper can say anything about the impending move, I pull the meat out of the oven and place it on the countertop with a flourish. "Why don't you all grab a wedge and sit down while I carve the tenderloin," I say, nodding to the dining room.

"I'll help you," Cooper says, stepping around Corinne and joining me by the food.

I nod and watch as Corinne loops her free arm through Alessandra's, asking her questions about her plans for Italy. I'm more grateful than ever for my wonderful sisters-in-law, and take a moment to plan my defense tactics for whatever Cooper plans to say while pretending to help me.

"Italy?" He leans on his elbows while watching me

carve the meat.

"I don't want to talk about it," I say, refusing to look him in the eye. Whether his worry is valid or not, there's no way I'm going to admit to it.

"What's the end game here, Quinn? I'd understand if you were just screwing around, but this? Joining us for Sunday dinner? Introducing her to your family? It seems like you're barreling down a road that leads nowhere."

I sigh and set the carving knife down on the counter. "I don't know, Coop. I'm just trying to spend time with her while I can."

At that, he softens, but before he can say anything else, I pick up the dish of sliced tenderloin in one hand and the roasted vegetables in the other and escape to the dining room.

I push all thoughts of Alessandra leaving out of my head. Now is not the time to go down that road.

I set the food on the table and take my seat next to Alessandra. "*Buon appetito*," I say, winking at her. She smiles and places her hand gently on my knee before taking the first bite of her meal.

As everyone starts eating, we chat about the recent renovations at the library where Emma works, as well as the new program she and Corinne are organizing with the library for the disabled community. The two of them are doing amazing things in the Boston area, and I can't be prouder to call them family.

"Speaking of work," Emma says after explaining the logistics of the program, "how's the Kingsley empire running these days?"

"Yeah, Quinn, I don't know how we haven't talked much about this yet, but I would love to know more about the world of dating services," Alessandra says, turning to me with a playful smile.

Cooper and Gavin stare at her for a moment, then turn to me with their brows raised.

"We run an escort service," Gavin says bluntly.

Ever the fucking charmer. I hoped to avoid this topic for a little while longer, since it can be like walking into a land mine.

"We provide high-end dates to wealthy clients. It's less a dating service and more a one-night thing," Cooper adds, trying to soften the details a bit.

"Oh, that sounds. . .interesting," Alessandra mumbles, taking a sip of her wine. I can tell from the look on her face that she's shocked, and I brace myself for a barrage of awkward questions.

Much to my surprise, she says nothing and lets the conversation drift off to the next topic. Even though she's cordial and polite for the rest of the meal, I can tell she's holding something back, and I resolve to talk to her about it later.

My brothers and their wives leave shortly after we finish eating. We all have work early tomorrow morning, and married life has moved their bedtimes significantly earlier.

As I shut the door behind them, I turn to find Alessandra standing nervously in the entryway, her purse slung over her shoulder.

"I don't want to keep you," she says, taking a step toward the door.

"Do you have to leave so soon?" I ask, stepping toward her. I can tell from the look on her face that she's overwhelmed, and while I want her to stay, I don't want to make her more uncomfortable.

"I just don't know what we're doing, Quinn," she says on a sigh. She adjusts the purse strap on her shoulder and looks down at the floor. "I saw the way your brothers looked at you when I told them I was going to Italy. I may be young, but I'm not stupid. Maybe they're right. Maybe this is all one huge mistake."

"Alessandra…" I reach out to take her hand, but she pulls away.

"I don't want to cause you any issues. I'm only here for a short time, and I…" She crosses her arms and leans away from me, her eyes suddenly dark and somber.

I step toward her, placing my hand on her cheek. "Stay, *per favore*," I whisper, hoping that an Italian *please* will be more effective than an English one.

Alessandra smiles softly, turning her face in my hand to place a small kiss on my palm.

"Besides," I say, pulling her into me and leading her to the kitchen, "I need help with all these dishes."

We wash the dishes in comfortable silence. As much

as I want to ask her what she thinks of my brothers and reassure her about our time together, I decide that giving her some time to relax will be helpful. Once the dishes are done, I pour us each another glass of wine and lead her to the living room.

We each take a seat on opposite ends of the couch, and after taking a sip of her wine, Alessandra looks at me expectantly.

"I'm sorry you were blindsided by the truth about our business," I say, ready to be more honest with her than ever. "It's not that I didn't want you to know, it's just. . .difficult to explain sometimes."

Alessandra nods and raises her eyebrows, prompting me to continue.

"As Cooper said, it's a high-end thing. Like when a CEO needs a date for a charity gala. A lot of these wealthy, powerful men are too busy to actually date, so we provide competent, attractive women for them to have on their arm. For a hefty fee, of course. We take excellent care of our girls, and make sure nothing bad happens to them."

Alessandra nods again, more slowly this time, clearly

thinking through what I just told her. "I'm fine with all that," she says. "I mean, no judgment here. It's just. . .you don't sleep with the women, do you?" She looks me in the eye then, her gaze wide and searching.

"No, never."

"How did you three get into this business? It seems like a very specific field to be working in."

I nod, sipping my wine while deciding what exactly to tell her. When I look over at her, I can see she isn't looking for a reason to judge or reprimand me. She wants to understand, that's all. I know in that very moment that this woman deserves to know the truth, so with a small sigh, I begin to explain my family history.

"Our father wasn't really around growing up, and it was hard for our mother with three boys. Eventually, she had to turn to less mainstream forms of employment. When things got bad, to put food on the table, she turned to prostitution. My brothers and I spent so many years protecting her and making sure that no one harmed her, that when she died so young. . .we sort of fell into this business. We knew that for some women, this was the only option, and if we weren't there to protect them, someone else would take advantage. So, we started Forbidden Desires. Growing up, we never thought our experiences with our mother would translate into a future business, but here we are, all these years later."

I shake my head as I finish my explanation, placing my hands in my lap. It isn't as painful to share as it once might have been, but I'm always a little nervous opening up to people.

Alessandra scoots next to me on the couch, taking my large hand in her small one and bringing it to her lips. She places a gentle kiss on the back of it, murmuring, "Thank you for opening up like that. I know how difficult that must have been because I imagine others may judge you for the services that you offer. Please know that I'm not that kind of person. Thank you for dinner. I had no idea you were such a good cook."

We both chuckle, and I pull her closer, staring into her eyes before bringing my lips to hers in a gentle kiss. She responds by parting her lips and slipping her tongue into my mouth, as she wraps her arms around me. Our breathing grows heavier and heavier, until Alessandra swings her leg around to straddle me on the couch, grinding her body into mine. And, *fuck*, it feels good.

My hands wander over her back and down to her perfect ass, running over it softly before giving both cheeks a firm squeeze. Alessandra responds by slipping her hands under my sweater, pressing her palms softly into my chest before running them down to my belt, which she slowly begins to unbuckle. As her hands unfasten my pants, she moves her mouth to my neck, nibbling softly upward until her lips brush against my earlobe, at which point she whispers, "I really hope you're going to take me to a nice restaurant soon."

As the words leave her mouth, she slips her hand inside my jeans to feel my throbbing cock through my briefs. I groan at her touch but shift my hips away from her, remembering what I told her about our first time.

"Soon." I groan, nuzzling into her neck and delighting in the soft moans each kiss draws out of her. "How about Thursday night?"

Alessandra pulls back for a moment, her hand still reaching for my erection, and asks, *"Our lesson?"*

"Instead of our regular lesson," I whisper, moving to nibble around her collarbone, "we could go to dinner. There's another great Italian restaurant I know. We'll go there to talk and to eat. . .it could be a good way to really immerse ourselves in the culture."

"As long as you let me order," she says, taking my face in both her hands and looking excitedly in my eyes. "You're an excellent cook, but I'm worried that your Italian will have us pairing red wine and fish."

"As my tutor, I believe that would be your fault," I say with a laugh.

"I can't help it if Sal let you develop bad habits."

"Sal might have let me get away with a few things, but he certainly never let me do this."

In one smooth motion, I flip Alessandra over onto her back lengthwise on the couch. She giggles, and her giggles quickly turn into moans as I move my mouth over her neck and use my fingers to elicit pleasure-filled sighs from her.

Even if tonight won't be our first time, I'm determined to make the most of my time with Alessandra before she gets on a plane and flies out of my life forever.

Chapter Seven

Alessandra

"Erica, I told you, we can't go outside until your brother is done eating," I say, lifting another spoonful of orange goop to baby Ben's lips. Veggie medley, I think.

Erica groans and throws herself on the floor, ever the drama queen. I do my best not to roll my eyes and focus on feeding the baby.

All right, Alessandra, nine hours down, one hour to go. There's a big plate of pasta and a hunky millionaire waiting for you at the end of this hell of a day.

Ben pulls his head away from the spoon, his tiny lower lip quivering with frustration. I try the old airplane trick one last time, trilling my lips and making the spoon look like it's flying, only to be met with another head jerk from the baby.

"Come on, Ben, open up," I croon, bringing the spoon to his lips again.

But the moment the goop touches Ben's mouth, he

shrieks in protest, pounding his little fists on the tray in front of him. Erica decides that now is a good time to start screaming over the sounds of her brother, asking me if it's time to leave for the park yet.

Some days, my nanny job is so smooth and simple, it makes me feel like I'm cheating the system.

Today is not one of those days. And the only thing getting me through today's nightmare is knowing that this is the night Quinn will finally be taking me out for a nice dinner. . .which means we'll finally get to do all the dirty things I've been fantasizing about since the first time I stumbled into his office.

Trying to salvage my sanity, I remind myself that I learned a long time ago that there's no use trying to yell over two screaming children, so instead, I sit quietly in my seat and wait for them to be done.

Erica finishes screaming first, tugging at the hem of her shorts and looking at me expectantly. I stick the spoon back in the jar of baby food and mix it around. He's already eaten half of it, and I decide he can be done.

"All right, Erica, I think your brother's done eating. Can you go get me his shoes? He's not quite ready to leave yet," I say in my calmest, most measured voice.

"I'll get Ben's shoooes!" Erica yells, turning and tearing around the corner to the coat closet.

I set the jar of baby food on the counter behind me and unbuckle Ben from his high chair. His little face breaks into a smile as I lift him from his chair, and he happily coos as I hold him on my hip. Erica returns to the kitchen, a tiny sneaker in each hand, and looks at me with wide, pleading eyes.

Before she can ask about the park again, my cell phone rings in my purse across the room. I carry Ben to the counter where my purse sits and pull out my phone, my spirits sinking at the sight of the name flashing on the screen.

"Hi, Lorraine, everything okay?" I ask, a knot forming in my stomach. *Don't do this to me, Lorraine. Not today. Any day but today.*

"Alessandra, hi. I'm so sorry, but I'm gonna be a couple hours late. Things at the office—son of a bitch, don't do this to me! Sorry, Alessandra, not you, this damn copy machine keeps jamming on me."

I close my eyes and try not to sigh. *Every fucking time I have somewhere important to be…*

"Alessandra, sweetie, did I lose you?" Lorraine's voice cuts through my thoughts.

"Sorry, I was just checking on Ben. That's fine, Lorraine, don't worry about it. Hope everything's all right on your end."

"Thanks, sweetie, you know I'll do my best to be home by eight. Nine, at the latest. Gotta go. Thanks, doll."

Fuck. I sigh and hang up the phone, placing it face down on the counter behind me.

"Was that Mommy?" Erica asks, sliding my phone toward her.

"Yes, that was Mommy," I reply, taking my phone from her sticky fingers. "She'll be home a little late tonight. And I told you, no playing with my phone without asking."

"Sorry," Erica mutters, looking down at her hands.

I look down at Ben, who's miraculously fallen asleep

against my shoulder. It's not his naptime, but with the way this day is going, I'm fine with letting him do what he wants.

"All right, Erica, I'm gonna put Ben down for his nap, then we can go play in the backyard until it's dark outside. Does that sound good?"

Her face lights up, and she nods enthusiastically. My heart sinks as I think of the dress I won't be wearing tonight and the delicious Italian food I won't be eating.

"And if you're really good," I add, gently patting Ben on the back, "we might even order a pizza tonight."

"Yaaay!" Erica cries, quickly clapping her hand over her mouth and staring at her brother. Luckily for us, Ben sleeps like a rock, and not even her excitement is enough to wake him.

As I lie Ben down in his crib, I check the clock on the wall. Four-thirty. I'm not looking forward to calling Quinn, but I know it needs to be done.

Walking back into the kitchen, I tell Erica that I'll meet her outside in a minute. She shrugs and sprints through the back door, itching to play in the sandbox

Lorraine had installed for her a couple of weeks ago. I try not to think about all the sand I'll have to sweep up later as I pull up Quinn's contact on my phone.

That knot in my stomach grows a little bigger as I press CALL and the line begins to ring.

"*Pronto.*" Quinn's voice chirps across the line, his cheery Italian greeting making me feel even worse about having to cancel. He even rolled the freaking *r* like the good Italian speaker he's quickly becoming.

"Hi, Quinn," I say, my tone giving away more than I mean it to.

"Everything okay?" he says, picking up on my hesitation. This would all be a lot easier if he weren't so attentive and kind.

"Yeah, everything's fine," I say, pacing around the kitchen island. "Well, not fine, really, but I'm okay. I, uh. . .I can't make it tonight, though. Lorraine's held up at work, so it looks like I'm stuck here longer than I thought I'd be tonight." *Just me and the freaking children from hell. Not exactly what I had planned for my evening.*

"Oh," Quinn says, and I can hear the hurt and

disappointment in his voice.

"I'm so sorry."

"No, don't be. It's not your fault."

"I know, but I just. . .I'm leaving in a couple weeks, and I was really looking forward to our date."

"Yeah, me, too. But if the kids need you…"

"Yeah, I guess I can't just leave them here on their own."

Quinn chuckles, but I feel a sad tension settling between us.

"Are you free tomorrow night?" I ask, reaching for something to communicate that I still want to see him. I know I have a good reason for not being able to make it, but I feel awful for having to cancel our date.

"Tomorrow night I have a work function," he says.

Well, shit, looks like we won't be fucking anytime soon after all.

"Would you like to join me?" Quinn asks. "It's a charity gala my brothers and I are invited to every year.

Cooper and Gavin can't make it, so I could use some company."

My stomach drops. *Didn't see that coming.*

"I'd love to." I don't think I have anything to wear, but now isn't the time to worry about it.

"Wonderful. I'll pick you up at eight."

"Okay, perfect." At that moment, I look out the window and see Erica sitting in the sandbox with her tongue out, slowly raising a handful of sand to her mouth. "Quinn? I gotta run. This little she-devil is about to eat dirt."

"Go save the day," he says with a chuckle. "I'll see you tomorrow night."

I tell Quinn good-bye and grab the baby monitor before running out the back door to stop Erica. My decision to stop her from eating sand sends her into a full-blown meltdown, just in time for baby Ben to wake up and start screaming in his crib.

I spend the next two hours playing zone defense, trying to calm both kids down long enough for their mom to get home.

• • •

By the time I finally make it home around eight o'clock that night, I make myself a sad ham-and-cheese sandwich and try not to think about the evening I missed out on.

I can't believe I had to cancel my date with Quinn tonight. Lorraine can be flaky, but of all the times for her to be late, this was definitely the worst.

Sandwich in hand, I make my way to my closet and push clothes around, looking for a dress fancy enough for a gala. Based on the suits Quinn wears to work, I suspect this event will be black tie.

Just when I resign myself to the fact that I'll need to go to the mall and get a fancy dress tomorrow, my doorbell rings. I frown and try to peek out my window to see who's at the door, but the angle isn't quite right for me to tell.

After setting my sandwich down on the table, I go to the door and open it to find a small man standing there with a large rectangular box in his hands.

"Delivery for Alessandra," the man says, holding the

box out to me.

Hesitantly, I take it from him, and he promptly turns and walks back to his car.

"Thank you!" I call after him and turn to figure out what the heck is going on. I take the box into the kitchen, where I use a pair of scissors to cut the ribbon across the top.

I open the box to find a note from Quinn sitting on top of something wrapped in off-white tissue paper.

Bellissima Alessandra,

Something for tomorrow night almost as beautiful as you.

Yours, Quinn

Intrigued, I rip through the tissue paper to find a gorgeous satin gown neatly folded in the box. I gasp and gently lift it out of the cardboard, relishing in the weight and silkiness of the fabric. The dress has thin straps and a small train, and an intricately beaded bodice.

As I gingerly hold the dress in my hands, excitement

builds within me. No one has ever done anything like this for me before, so sweet and thoughtful. I lay the dress carefully over the chair in the corner of my room, afraid that my cheap hangers will hurt it.

Inside the box, beneath the dress is the most exquisite pair of heels, in my size, that match perfectly with the dress. I can't help but slip my feet into them and parade around my bedroom.

I can tell already that my date with Quinn tomorrow will be one of the most special nights of my life.

Chapter Eight

Quinn

Stretching my hands up into the air, I lean back in my chair and take a deep breath as I check the clock on the wall of my office for the fifth time today. Three forty-five.

Damn.

A few more houres, that's all I have to get through. A few more hours, and I'll be in the same room as Alessandra. I'll get to stare into her brown eyes, feel the warmth of her skin, take in every inch of her perfect curves.

I remember the dress I picked out for her, and a smile rises to my lips. It's almost as gorgeous as her. I can't wait to see her in it.

A notification pops up on my screen to remind me about the gala tonight, and I lean forward to click it away. My brothers and I have taken turns attending this gala for years now, and I don't need any reminders about the dress code or the philanthropies it benefits. As I scan my computer screen, one thing stands out to me. . .today's date.

Alessandra leaves in two weeks.

Fuck.

I take another deep breath, pushing away from my desk and standing up. After a brief moment of panic, a wave of resolve washes over me. I have two weeks. *What the fuck do I have to lose?*

I'm going all in, pulling out all the stops. I decide then and there that if I do nothing else in the two weeks before she leaves, I'm going to full-on woo Alessandra.

My mind races with ideas, thoughts of all the things I want to do for and to this beautiful young woman threatening to overwhelm me. I haven't felt this strongly about a woman since. . .well, ever, and it's clear to me now that I have no choice but to give this relationship everything I have. Even if she leaves me in the end, I have to be able to say that I did everything in my power to keep her.

Suddenly, my thoughts are interrupted by a quick knock on the door. Before I can say anything, Cooper comes waltzing into my office wearing a smug smile. Ever since meeting Alessandra at our family dinner on Sunday, he's been trying to give me shit about her. Aware of his obnoxious tendencies, I've been successful at avoiding him all week, but it seems he finally gave in to his annoying urges, literally cornering me in my office to tease me.

"How can I help you?" I sigh, ready to get this conversation over with as soon as possible.

"We never got a chance to chat after dinner on Sunday, brother," Cooper says with a grin.

I know there's no malice in his teasing, but I'm not in the mood to hear what he has to say. "Didn't think there was much to talk about, *brother*."

"Ah, well, I just have a few questions, really, after watching you with Alessandra."

I lean back in my chair. "Shoot."

Cooper takes a seat in one of the chairs opposite my desk, taking a moment to settle in, his legs spread wide and his hands folded over his stomach. He lifts his chin, a mischievous smile on his face. "First question, and arguably the most important one, how's twenty-two-year-old pussy?"

As the words leave Cooper's mouth, I bristle, quickly rising from my seat and marching to the door. "Get out," I spit out, opening the door and gesturing for him to leave.

Cooper stands, raising his hands in surrender. "Oh, come on, Quinn, it's a valid question. I haven't fucked a twenty-two-year-old in years."

I don't respond, simply growl and motion for him to leave again.

"Wait a second," he says, his hands dropping to his sides. "You don't know, do you? Why else would you be so tense about this? Unless you're in love with her or something, but we both know it's too soon for that."

Cooper's words hit me right in the chest, knocking the wind out of me for a second. I quickly recover, clenching my jaw and crossing my arms, but it's too late. He saw me falter, and there's no use denying anything. Whether I like it or not, both of my brothers can see right through me.

But that doesn't mean I have to talk to either of them

about it.

"Out," I say, jerking my head toward the open door.

Cooper sighs. "Fine, I'll leave you alone. But don't think for one second you're off the hook here, man."

He brushes past me and walks out the door. I shut the door behind him, my blood still boiling in frustration. I can't tell if I'm mad at Cooper, exactly, or if I'm just upset hearing him point out the things I've barely been able to admit to myself.

I check the clock again. Four o'clock. I gather my things, flip off the lights, and walk out of my office, closing the door behind me. As I march through the building, I run into Gavin and Alyssa, who both give me inquisitive looks.

"Going somewhere?" Gavin asks, eyeing the briefcase in my hand.

"Home," I answer gruffly, sidestepping him to get to the exit.

"Are you sick?" Alyssa asks after me, her eyes wide. "You haven't left the office this early in ten years."

"Fine," I say over my shoulder, quickly pushing through the door and walking to my car.

I don't care if they think something's wrong. All I want in this moment is to get home and get ready for the gala. I haven't been able to think about anything but Alessandra all day, and I don't think an extra hour or two of pretending to work would do anyone any good.

• • •

When I get home, I shower, then towel-dry my hair and shave. My getting-ready routine is simple, but more than anything, I want time to take it slow and sort my thoughts.

As I leave my hair to air-dry before styling it with pomade, I dress in the new suit I ordered for this occasion. It's classic, simple, but it fits perfectly and serves as an ideal complement to Alessandra's gown. I finish my hair and dab on a bit of my signature cologne, giving myself one last once-over in the mirror.

I call the limo driver, and he tells me he'll be in front of my house in five minutes. When the limo arrives, I chat briefly with the driver before climbing into the backseat. It feels strange sitting in the back of a limo alone, but I use the ride as an opportunity to go over my plans for the evening in my mind.

I know from our previous social outings that Alessandra will be fine. I'm not worried about her fitting in and keeping up in conversations in the slightest. We'll eat good food, drink superb champagne, and schmooze with wealthy socialites. I already know the looks I'll receive from the other men at the gala, who will most likely assume that Alessandra is one of my escorts, and I can't wait to revel in their surprise when they learn how accomplished and competent she is.

For as excited as I am to see Alessandra and show her off to a roomful of rich, stuffy people, the thought of our first time being intimate looms large in the back of my mind. Just thinking of it now makes my cock twitch, and I can only imagine how needy it will be by the end of the night.

Before my fantasies can progress any further, the limo pulls up in front of Alessandra's apartment. I climb out of the backseat and walk to her door, my stomach churning as I ring the doorbell. I feel a little silly for feeling so nervous, but I can't help it. I've been eager to see her all day, and now that it's finally happening, I can't contain my excitement.

Within moments, the door opens and she's standing in front of me.

Holy fuck. She looks even more gorgeous than I ever thought possible.

The gown fits her perfectly, the beaded bodice hugging her shapely breasts just right so the rest of the fabric can cascade gently over her body. Her dark, luxurious hair is pulled back into a neat bun, leaving a few curls to fall gracefully around her face. She's absolutely stunning.

I stare at her for a few seconds too long, my mouth slightly open, and only a soft "ahem" from Alessandra pulls me out of my stupor.

"I'm sorry." I run my hand over my face. "I don't even know what to say."

Alessandra steps out onto the stoop, closing the door behind her. Her eyes are wide and frantic, and she immediately begins patting at her hair.

"Don't know what to say in a good way, right? I've

never worn anything this fancy. I can't tell if it's working or if I look freaking ridiculous," she says in a rush, shifting her weight from one foot to the other.

I chuckle softly and take her hand in mine. "You look perfect." Our eyes meet, and she gives me a grateful smile. "More than perfect, actually. Every woman at this thing will hate you."

"Shut up," she says, laughing and playfully hitting my stomach. "Wait, are you serious? Is it too much?"

"Rilassati," I whisper, leaning down to place a soft kiss on her cheek. *Relax.* "You'll only stand out in the sense that you'll be the most beautiful woman there."

Alessandra lifts her chin and places her lips on mine. When we part, I beat her to the joke we usually share. "We better stop before your lipstick gets all over us."

She laughs and playfully hits me again.

"Shall we?" I offer my arm. She loops her hand gently through it, and the two of us make our way to the limo.

The ride to the gala goes by faster than I anticipated. Alessandra and I spend the whole time talking, first about our work week, and then about, well, everything. Talking with her is one of my favorite things to do.

After tonight, however? I have a feeling I'll discover a new favorite thing to do with her.

When we arrive at the venue, she loops her arm through mine again, and the two of us make our grand entrance together. The gala is planned by one of our clients, so I give Alessandra a quick rundown of who we'll be mingling with for the evening. She nods along silently, and I can't help but notice how much calmer she looks in this moment than she did when I was telling her about my brothers. She's a fast learner, and I can already tell she'll be an amazing date.

Once inside the ballroom, we pause to survey the room. A waiter walks by with a tray of champagne, and Alessandra and I each take a flute. We gently clink glasses and take a sip.

"This is the best champagne I've ever had in my life," she whispers, looking at me with wide, approving eyes.

I smile. "I've had better."

Alessandra smiles back, poking her elbow into my

ribs. Before she can give me her witty response, I make eye contact with one of our clients, who waves us over to him.

"All right, *bellissima*, let the schmoozing begin," I say softly in her ear, placing my hand on her lower back as we make our way across the room to the client.

"Quinn!" the client says jovially, clapping his hand on the side of my arm. "I was wondering which of the Kingsley brothers would make it tonight. So good to see you. And who is this charming creature on your arm?" The client turns his appraising gaze to Alessandra, extending his hand to her and raising his eyebrows.

"Glen Williams, I'd like you to meet Alessandra. Alessandra, this is Mr. Williams," I say, nodding between the two.

"Call me Glen, please."

"It's a pleasure, Glen," she says, placing her hand in his and bowing her head ever so slightly.

I can tell by the look on Glen's face that he thinks Alessandra is one of our Forbidden Desires girls, so I say, "Alessandra is our company's Italian expert. She's fluent, and she's been trying to teach me, but I'm afraid I'm a terrible student."

"*Your Italian is good,*" Alessandra says to me with a smile.

"*My teacher is good,*" I reply.

Alessandra smiles up at me, and the two of us lock eyes. For a moment, I forget that we're among other people.

"*Non vedo l'ora di stare da solo con te,*" I murmur, my gaze wandering over her body. *I can't wait to be alone with you.*

The smile fades a bit from Alessandra's lips, and her eyes smolder with desire, the softest catch of her breath, so slight that only I can hear. She raises an eyebrow ever so slightly, and my cock twitches in response. A wave of pure lust washes over me, and it takes every ounce of my self-restraint to keep from ripping the dress off Alessandra's body and ravishing her right here and now.

"*Bravo!*" Glen says, snapping me out of my fantasy.

I take in a quick breath and turn to smile genially at him, then ask about his business.

As Glen drones on about market prices and rises in stock, I feel Alessandra move closer to me, the heat of her body warming my side. With her hand still on my arm, she rubs her thumb over my bicep, and all I can think of is her hands running over my shaft, the warmth of her mouth as she takes every inch of me inside it. I steal a quick glance at her face, only to find her smiling and nodding at Glen, seemingly unaware of the effect she's having on me. This makes me want her even more, and I can't wait until this gala is over.

Glen eventually excuses himself from our conversation, pointing out a colleague he needs to see across the room. Alessandra and I continue milling around the event, chatting with other clients and attendees, enjoying hors d'oeuvres, and showing off our Italian banter. Alessandra, as usual, is incredible the whole night, dazzling everyone we talk to with her grace and charm. Even though I knew she would handle the event beautifully, by the end of the night, I'm in awe of how well she fits in.

As the gala winds down, I place my hand on the small of her back and lean down to whisper in her ear. "What do you say we get out of here," I murmur, letting my lips softly brush her earlobe.

A small grin flashes across her face as she turns and lifts her chin so her lips are merely inches from mine. "Thought you'd never ask…and just so you know, I'm counting this as an old-fashioned date with dinner and getting dressed up," she replies, her gaze wandering to my mouth. I'm about to lean in to kiss her when she pulls away, taking my hand in hers and leading me outside.

Such a little tease.

I follow behind her, enjoying the view of her round, voluptuous ass.

The limo arrives to take us to my place within minutes, and the two of us climb into the back. I close the door and settle in beside Alessandra, and then I lean my face to hers, taking her mouth in an eager, passionate kiss. She responds, kissing me back, swirling her tongue against mine. Caught up in the moment, I lift her on top of me, hiking her dress up over her hips so my hands can more easily wander over her legs and ass. The heels she's wearing giving me a visual fantasy I can't wait to explore later.

With her straddling me, I move my mouth to her neck and collarbone, and small moans escape from her. Damn, she's so sexy and responsive. My need for her grows with each heartbeat. My cock now pressing firmly into her thigh, I move my hands to her breasts, squeezing them before teasing her fully erect nipples.

We're both breathing heavily now, Alessandra's little moans escaping even more frequently. I can't wait until we arrive at my place.

Moving her to the seat next to me, I push her dress up even farther, the fabric gathering around her waist. I move to my knees before her, trailing my tongue from one thigh to the other, gently biting the soft, supple skin near her sex.

Before I even touch them, I can tell that her panties are soaked all the way through. My cock gives another eager twitch, as if to remind me that he's there and he's been so damn patient. With both hands on her thighs, I use my teeth to pull her lacy thong away from her hips, letting my teeth graze her skin a little harder than they did before. Alessandra glances at the screen that prevents the driver from seeing us, then lifts her hips to help me.

Once I slip her panties over her ankles, I ball them in my hand and sit back for a moment to fully take her in. She's fully on display, her legs spread, pussy glistening, chest heaving in anticipation.

She's perfect.

So pink and tight and wet.

"*Per favore,*" she whispers between breaths, arching her back and splaying her legs even wider apart. *Please.*

Without hesitation, I descend on her, placing rough, needy kisses along her silken, wet core. She immediately groans in response, bucking her hips into me. I run my tongue over the length of her, lapping at her, loving how responsive and vocal she is.

Just as she approaches the brink of climax, I sit up, bringing my face to hers to pull her into another passionate kiss. She lets out a small, frustrated moan, but before it can even finish, I thrust two fingers inside her, swirling my thumb over her clit as I pump my fingers. Her frustrated moan becomes a pleasure-filled cry.

Alessandra gasps, throws her head back, and I take the opportunity to suck and bite around the base of her neck. Within moments, a series of moans erupt from her as she comes on my hand. It's so fucking sexy.

As her moans fade to whimpers, the limo slows to a stop. I lift my lips to her ear and whisper, "*Bellissima*, we're here."

Chapter Nine

Alessandra

The door clicks shut behind my back as Quinn pushes me against it. I had an amazing time with him tonight, which is no surprise because I always enjoy his company, but what he just did to me in the limo—his mouth moving over me like that—proves he's so much more incredible and way more experienced than I deserve.

My coat falls to the floor in a puddle as Quinn runs his fingers under the straps of my dress, lightly massaging the muscles of my back and neck. His warm hands are a welcome buffer between my skin and the cool door. Quinn Kingsley is ever the gentleman, seeing to my comfort—and to my pleasure—before his own. And there's no mistaking his bulging manhood, which is pressing into my belly.

I bite down on his lip, trying to tame the girlish smile threatening to give away my infatuation with this creature. He groans, and I swear I could die on the spot and be a happy girl. This man, with his firm, muscled body under my searching hands. This man, with his tongue tangling with mine in a hot, powerful kiss. This man, whose self-control is driving me a little bit mad.

As soon as I can free him from his shirt, that bare, chiseled chest is under my palms. I claim it with my fingernails, dragging them lightly down his chest, feeling the soft hair there. I need to see him. I push him away from me, giving myself just enough space to really get a good look.

Quinn Kingsley stands before me in all his sexy, indescribable glory. His tie is loose around his neck and his shirt is half-open from my impatient tugging. His face is flushed, his eyes dark and clouded with lust.

Impatient with my scrutiny, Quinn tries to step back into my arms but I hold him there—on display. I want to see him, to soak in the sight before me, to run my gaze up and down the angles and contours that have quickly become my new obsession. His stomach is lined with muscles, and his chest is broad and firm with sexy pectorals. He looks every bit a man.

I have never been this wet for anyone in my life.

"What?" He sounds gruff, clearly grieving the loss of

contact. "Why do you laugh?"

I didn't even realize that I was.

"I want—" I try to conjure up words for the wild, twisting desire I have for him, but find I'm unable to. "I want—"

Speechless, I drag my hands down his chest again, as if I can find the words somewhere in the inspiration of his perfectly toned abs. He grins at me then, covering my hands with his and drawing me close.

"You want…" His lips brush along my temple, the warmth of his breath stealing mine away.

I may faint. I've got to take control. In one swift tug, I rip off his shirt and tie and toss them on my discarded coat. The surprise on his face makes me feel stronger and more experienced than I am.

"You and me. On your bed. *Adesso*." Now.

Quinn is on me in seconds.

Are my feet even on the floor? No, his arms are holding me up, one under my legs, the other securely behind my back. I kick off my shoes with a flourish and wrap my arms around his neck, weaving my fingers through his hair as he carries me across his apartment.

A moment later, I'm lowered gently onto the plushest, silkiest bedspread I've ever felt. The reminder of Quinn's lavish lifestyle doesn't escape me. *How did I end up here? How did this exquisite Adonis of a man—*

I must have a perplexed look on my face because he tilts his head in concern. *Shut up, Alessandra, and be with this man who wants to be with you.*

I give him a smile—full, open, and honest. "Come here," I say, my arms outstretched for him.

He smiles at me, almost with an uncharacteristically boyish sincerity. His body arches over me on the bed, one hand propping himself up while the other cups my cheek.

"*Never. Stop. Smiling,*" he commands me, punctuating each word with a soft kiss.

I pull him closer to me with what can only be described as a purr. He's more than happy to oblige.

The sensation of silky sheets doesn't compare to the feeling of Quinn's half-naked body sliding up against mine. I immediately spread my legs so he can stake his claim on the space between them. We fit perfectly together. His lips find mine again, and every firm grind of his pelvis against mine makes me want to be even closer.

"Take it off," I plead, tugging at his belt.

He groans. "*Pazienza.*" *Patience.*

"No more patience," I whisper in his ear. One of my hands feverishly combs through his hair while the other slides over the front of his pants, grasping his manhood greedily.

He grunts as I slide my hand over him. "Take off your dress." It's a command, not a question.

I rise to my knees on the bed, unzipping my dress. When I let it fall away, I'm left in only a scrap of lace. Time comes to a stop as Quinn's hot gaze rakes over my skin, and he groans.

"Jesus. You're exquisite."

I swallow a wave of nerves. No one has ever described me that way. But here, on his bed, in the moonlight, I feel beautiful. Maybe it's the way he looks at me, but I really do feel like the most exquisite woman in the world.

"Your turn," I whisper, reaching for his belt. I give it a tug and Quinn seems amused, pleased to just watch me as I undo his button and then tug down his zipper.

Now there's nothing separating me from his cock, and a fresh wave of hot, nervous passion crashes over me. This is it. I've never been more excited to get in someone's pants as I am now.

As I peel down his boxer briefs, Quinn watches me with the patience of a saint. I know he must be as eager as I am—the fabric at the front of his boxers is barely accommodating the most mouth-watering erection I've ever seen.

He shudders as I pull him out of the constraint of his boxers. He's huge. And perfect. And so incredibly hot and solid in my hand.

Grasping him low on the shaft, I pull him toward me, feeling the length of him. I lean in, kissing him softly. With every stroke, I suck on his lower lip. The sheets tighten around my shoulders as he digs his fingers into the silk. As tension builds in his shoulders, I feel a desperation mounting to take him inside me.

His hair is a mess, a sexy fucking wondrous mess of

perfect, soft locks. I dig my fingers into it, pulling his gaze from my hand on his cock to my eyes. I want him looking at me when I run my thumb over the pre-cum beading on his eager tip. Those chocolate-brown eyes shutter closed with pleasure as the broad tip of him presses against my wet underwear. The electricity that thrums through me, through us, makes us both bite our lips to silence our groans. We smile at our shared reactions.

"*Tu sei il diavolo.*" *You're the devil.* The look of adoration in his smiling eyes tells me he thinks quite the opposite.

"*Come?*" I blink innocently back at him. *How?*

"You feel too good to be anything but *peccaminoso,*" he says with a sigh. *Sinful.* The bilingual phrasing is charming as hell. I definitely have taken a toll on this man's concentration.

I breathe hotly against his ear. "I want you."

He pulls my hand away from its repeated motions and places it above my head. The gesture is gentle, but is the action of a man who wants his turn.

"*Bellissima,* you shall have me." He whispers this into

the curve of my neck and shoulder.

Goose bumps cover my body. Rather than the confident seductress I was a moment ago, now I'm suddenly twenty-two again, at the mercy of an erotic power I'm more than happy to bend to. Quinn Kingsley can have me any way he goddamn pleases.

His lips trace down my neck, down my chest, stopping over my heaving breasts. He runs a finger over the hardened tip of my nipple, teasing.

At his touch, my back curves involuntarily. I whimper softly as the sensation runs down from my breast, straight to my pulsing core. Every time a guy touched my breasts in the past, it was like a watching a child mash potatoes with his bare hands. But this—this adoration with which he circles his finger around the sensitive tip, the sigh before he closes his lips around it— this is something else entirely.

" *Perfection*," he whispers..

I have to hold back a yelp when he licks a slow, torturous circle around my nipple and then sucks it into his mouth. My hips dig into his torso, grinding against him, dying for more friction.

"So good," I say in lazy English. "It feels so good."

"*Sei bravo.*" *You are good.*

The Italian phrase is simple, but it nearly brings tears to my eyes. He kisses an urgent line down the skin of my belly, his hands running down my legs to peel my sopping excuse for underwear away, and his lips are back on my pussy in seconds. I'm still taken aback by the luxury of having a man want to pleasure me so desperately. He sucks on the sensitive flesh between my legs with a hum that speaks of intense enjoyment.

"Quinn…" I moan, alternating between his name and unintelligible groans. His tongue dips into my clenching, throbbing entrance, and I shudder.

My eyes flutter open and I dare to look at him, feasting on me. His gaze is pinned on me, all the while he plants deep, meaningful kisses onto my most intimate of spots. In the limo, it was sheer lust, a wild thrill of passion. In Quinn Kingsley's bed, it's a slow burn with each press of his lips against me.

I bend my knees, opening myself more to his needy mouth. My bare feet slide from his back to his shoulders, where they dig into the muscles there. His hands slide from my hips to beneath me, cupping my ass and tenderly lifting my lower body off the bed. Feverish, I pull at the sheets around me, unable to stop my hips from thrusting up and down in time with every suck, lave, and twirl.

Already I can feel my orgasm boiling to the surface, and a thought occurs to me. . .this time, I want him to feel me come around him. I want him to feel the ecstasy rip through me and give him the satisfaction of a job well-fucking-done.

"Mr. Kingsley," I say on a gasp. "Would you—join—me?"

He knows exactly what I mean. With one last kiss to my quivering flesh, he lowers my pelvis back to the sheets and stands at the foot of the bed, naked and perfect. His massive erection glistens with a single dripping line of pre-cum. I want to lick it off him. I sit up, finding strength despite my dizziness. He grabs a condom from the bedside table and joins me back on the bed, kneeling between my parted knees.

"*Take me*," I murmur.

With my hand on his thick, uncovered cock, I guide

him where I need him. His tip rubs up and down against me, but doesn't enter.

"I'm on the pill," I tell him with a playful lift of my eyebrows. "I hope you're..."

"Squeaky clean," he says immediately.

His cock feels so hot and large between my legs, and I make a wordless sound of pleasure as he teases me with just the tip of him.

"Fuck." He groans. "So tight." His voice is rough, and the sound of it makes me clench around him.

Then my Italian stallion slides into me in one powerful thrust, and with just that one motion, I'm pretty sure he's ruined me for every other man.

Chapter Ten

Quinn

Even as I lean over her, my mouth inches from her, her legs wrapped around my waist, I can't believe Alessandra is in my bed.

Pumping my aching cock in and out of her perfectly tight pussy, I bring my mouth to her neck, nibbling gently at the soft skin below her ear. She moans softly, raising her hips to pull me deeper into her, then moaning again as I run my thumb over her stiff, rosy nipple. I can't get enough of the sounds she's making, and I decide to do everything I can to make her even more vocal.

Moving my mouth farther up her neck, I take her earlobe between my lips, sucking gently before grazing it with my teeth. Alessandra responds by bucking her hips again and raking her fingernails over my back. The sensation sends a perfect chill down my spine, and my cock responds with an eager pulse inside her.

I haven't felt this good—this happy—in a long time. Months, maybe years, if I'm being honest.

I can feel myself already approaching the brink of orgasm, but I'm not yet ready for our lovemaking to be over. I have to slow my pace, pumping into her with long, deep thrusts.

"Yes," she says, moaning at the change in tempo.

Moving my hands to either side of her head, I push myself up, my arms fully extended, and let my gaze wander lazily over her curves.

"Like that?" I push in deeply before slowly retreating again.

She bites her lip, her eyes fluttering closed briefly. "Yes."

"That will make you come?"

"Fuck," is all she says, but I'm pretty sure that's a yes. I continue the slow movements, pressing into her until I can't go any farther, and then retreat. Her moans change, coming faster, and I can't help but pump harder.

Alessandra groans and reaches for my face, touching my cheek. I comply, leaning down to kiss her.

"It's so good. You're perfect," I tell her, and she

moans again.

Fitting snugly inside her warm, throbbing pussy, I never want this to end, but once again, my cock reminds me how very ready he is to explode. My dick has reached critical mass and has been ever so patient with waiting.

Reaching a hand between us, I move my thumb rhythmically over her engorged clit. Alessandra arches her back instantly, moaning louder than before.

Holding on to her hip, I bury myself inside her, my pace quickening taking us both on the ride of our lives. We come within seconds of each other.

As the waves of orgasm wash over us both, I lower my body to Alessandra's, holding her close against me as her body spasms eventually fade.

After cleaning her up, I return to the bed. I lie on my back and Alessandra nestles into my side, resting her head on my chest. Wrapping my arms around her, I place tender kisses on her head and cheeks while she softly traces my pecs with her fingers.

"That was. . .amazing," she whispers, running her index finger over my sternum.

"*Sì*," I murmur in agreement, pulling her even closer to me.

We lie there for a moment, and eventually, Alessandra raises her head to look at me, resting her chin on me.

"It's getting late. I should probably head home soon," she says, turning to the bedside table to check the time. Once she finds the clock, she immediately turns back to me. "Your clock is wrong."

"No, it's not."

Alessandra lifts an eyebrow and props herself up on an elbow. "There's no way we just had sex for over an hour."

Placing an arm behind my head, I smirk. "We did."

She doesn't respond, simply stares at me, her mouth hanging open.

"It's called stamina," I tease. "Maybe there are some perks to being with an older man."

"There are many perks to being with you," she says, her eyes wide with disbelief, as she reaches down to grab my semi-erect cock that seems to be well on its way to starting round two.

Wanting to draw out our time together, I vow to keep her here all night.

"You know what else is incredible? Post-sex snacks." I place a final kiss on Alessandra's brow before sitting up and stretching my back.

"Mmm, *perfecto*," she murmurs, stretching before sitting up and swinging her legs over the edge of the bed.

I go to my closet and pull on a pair of boxers, then grab a shirt for Alessandra. I come back into the bedroom and toss her the shirt. She accepts it gratefully, pulling the soft fabric over her body and standing to join me.

We wander into the kitchen, where I pour us each a small glass of wine, then pull some cheese out of the fridge for us to snack on.

"Pita chips or Mediterranean flaxseed crackers?" I ask from the pantry.

"Pita chips," she calls.

"Pita, it is," I say, grabbing a bag and joining her in

the kitchen. "Not even a hint of hesitation?" I ask, teasing her for her quick response.

"I'm a woman who knows what she wants," she murmurs, leaning in and placing a soft kiss on my lips.

I return the kiss, taking a step closer to her, but before the kiss can turn into anything else, Alessandra backs away and pops a piece of cheese into her mouth.

"Priorities." She winks, taking her glass of wine and the plate of cheese into the living room.

I smile and shake my head. *This woman will be the death of me.*

Taking my glass of wine in one hand and the pita chips in the other, I follow Alessandra. I set our snacks down on the coffee table in front of the couch, then make my way to the record player in the corner of the room. After putting on my favorite record, I join her on the couch, smiling at how naturally she fits into my side, how right it feels to have my arm around her.

"*Buono?*" I ask, nodding to her wine. *Is it good?*

She nods. "*Molto bene, grazie.*" *Very good, thank you.*

I take another sip of my wine, my thoughts wandering to the topic I've been avoiding since the moment I met her.

"So," I say, mustering all the strength within me, "why Italy? I understand the desire to visit, but what made you decide to move there?"

Alessandra nods, sipping her wine before beginning. "Well, I've always kind of been obsessed with the Mediterranean. I'm a bit of a nerd like that. I've just always wanted to go and spend a good amount of time in Italy, especially. Once it became clear that my classics degree wasn't opening many doors for me stateside, I figured now was as good a time as any to just move and try building a life there."

"What do you hope to do?"

"Good question." She chuckles, then pauses, a slightly more serious look washing over her face. "I'm going to teach English. But who knows, I might just end up making espresso at a café or something."

I nod along, a thousand thoughts racing through my head. *Teach here. Make espresso here. Just stay.*

But instead of voicing any of those thoughts, I ask, "How long will you stay there?"

Alessandra doesn't respond for a moment. She takes a long sip of her wine, then a small, sad smile spreads across her face. "Indefinitely," she murmurs.

I nod again, a hollow feeling in the pit of my stomach. I know she's told me this before, but hearing her say the words again, after everything that's happened between us, sends my thoughts into a tailspin. The fact that she's leaving the country, might never come back, might meet someone else, might never curl up with me on this couch again. . .it's clearer to me in this moment than it ever was before.

I'm falling for this woman, whether I want to or not.

"I'm happy for you," I say, forcing my lips into a smile. I quickly pop another piece of cheese into my mouth to avoid saying anything I might regret, and rack my brain for something else to talk about. "So, tell me more about your nanny job. How did you find the family?"

Alessandra smiles and launches into the story behind

her job, but I can tell from her slight hesitation that she sees right through me. Thankfully, she doesn't seem to want to talk about her leaving any more than I do, and we spend the rest of the night chatting and snacking and drinking our wine, and it's perfect.

But through it all, I continually remind myself that my time with Alessandra is quickly coming to an end, whether I think she's perfect for me or not.

And when our time is up, I will be absolutely crushed.

Chapter Eleven

Alessandra

When I wake up, I'm cuddled against Quinn's sleeping form. We're entwined on the couch, his head tucked into the crook of my neck and his arms wrapped around my torso. I lift my head and find it's still dark outside. We must have fallen asleep, talking about everything from me being a nanny to him being co-owner of an escort service and all of the insanity that ensues in both of our day-to-day jobs.

A blush warms my cheeks. How long did I talk? I was so comfortable. . .. It must have been over an hour before we both dozed off from the wine.

With a cringe, I recall telling Quinn about the time Ben threw up on me at the park, otherwise known as the most humiliating moment of Erica's life. I think I even reenacted the completely bereft expression on her face when I approached her at the monkey bars, covered in baby puke, and told her in front of her new friends that we were going home. Quinn's chuckles fueled me as I described the melodrama of her tears and vows to *never, and I mean NEVER,* speak to me again. Since when is *that* a good post-sex story?

My embarrassment subsides as I look at his sleeping face. He liked the story. He likes me. He may more than like me.

How much do I like him?

Quinn's eyes flutter open, as if I had asked the question aloud.

"*What time is it?*" he asks. His voice is rough in that sexy, just-woken-up way. Oh God, do I like that voice.

"*It's late, I don't know,*" I whisper.. More so, I don't care. Time isn't on my mind when there are these long eyelashes to count and those cheekbones to powder with kisses.

"I do have a bed," he whispers back.

"Oh." I smile. "I remember that bed. You should show it to me again."

He smiles for the briefest of moments before burying his face in my neck and planting the warmest, sweetest kiss there. I squeeze him hard, bursting with feeling. With matching sighs, we lift our lazy bodies from the couch and shuffle back toward his room, my arm wrapped around his waist, his around my shoulder. He plants a kiss on my hair as our bare feet pad across the cold floors.

Under his plush covers, my feet instantly find warmth. He curls his body around mine, spooning me without the usual awkwardness of finding a comfortable position with another body in bed. Again, I take a moment to marvel about how well we fit together. I push my ass flirtatiously against his groin. Why not?

"Can I help you??" he murmurs.

"Maybe we can help each other," I murmur back in my sexiest, honey-sweet voice.

Quinn growls into my ear and nips at my earlobe. I giggle uncontrollably, and we're at it again.

This time, the sex is slow and warm. His one free hand cups my breast, massaging my nipple before running his fingers up and down my belly. The other hand I refuse to let go of, planting wet, tender kisses on each knuckle. Cocooned so tightly together, with his torso pressed against my back, it's easy to find a lazy, comfortable pace. Our climax is a slow, heavy burn, rocking us back and forth in indescribable bliss.

"*Grazie*," he says softly against the back of my sweat-soaked neck, half-asleep from the power of his orgasm. I hum contentedly in response, sated and ready for a restful sleep.

• • •

A hand stroking my hair wakes me the following morning. Quinn, fully dressed, crouches in front of me next to the bed, brushing what I can only assume is a rat's nest back from my face.

"*Buongiorno, stella marina*," he says, his eyes glimmering with amusement.

Starfish?

Then I realize the position I'm in. I'm sprawled across the bed, my hair wild and my legs twisted in the satin sheets. Realizing I'm not exactly at my most elegant, I groan.

"It's early," he says kindly.

I moan into the pillow. "Young people need more sleep."

"Are you calling me old?" He gasps quietly in mock offense. "So rude, when I've brought you…"

His hand roams over to the bedside table to reach for something, and my nose catches up to my grumbling stomach. I nearly squeal at the sight of freshly brewed coffee in a ceramic mug.

"You can't be serious." I'm almost in tears. It tastes so good. Like if Quinn Kingsley were a flavor, this would be it. My eyelids flutter in ecstasy.

"I'd like to take you out to breakfast once you're done making love to that cup." He chuckles.

"I've only got the dress I wore last night, though. Hello, walk of shame." Am I pouting? I may be, but missing out on a chance at breakfast with him is a somber thought.

"As much as I would love to see you in that dress again, I did think of that," he says with a smile. "I asked my assistant to pick up some necessities. It's all in the bathroom. Take your time. But not too long."

He plants a quick kiss on my still-pouting lips as I process all that he just said. Did he really think of everything? Is that possible?

I find my answer in his pristine master bath. On the marble countertop, I peruse through a pair of leggings, a pair of jeans, a simple tee shirt, a sweater, several styles of underwear, and even a bra *in my size.* I have options to choose from, all in a lovely array of colors that look as though they belong in my own closet.

I pop open the glass shower door and peek inside. Shampoos, shower gels, conditioner, and—is that a loofah?

A man who knows the luxury of a loofah is not to be replaced. This time, my inner voice sounds a lot like Deanna.

As the hot steam envelops me in the shower, I find my mind wandering.

Will I ever find anyone as incredible as Quinn again? In a foreign country, no less? The questions sneak up on me like an unwelcome poke in the back.

I try to shake off the nagging feeling that I already know the answers, and they aren't the answers that I want in this moment. I still have my whole life ahead of me. I forcibly draw my thoughts to my travel plans—my go-to thought bubble in moments of uncertainty. I scrub these thoughts into my skin, willing myself to focus on the plan. I will see places I've only read of, eat foods I've only attempted to recreate, and explore a variety of romantic endeavors with suitors I've only dreamed of.

I stop scrubbing so ferociously and stand perfectly still under the water, letting the liquid heat pour down on me. A final question lingers, a lingering of doubt at my periphery.

How many of those make-believe suitors will ever live up to Quinn?

• • •

In the café, I order another cup of coffee and a simple plate of pancakes with syrup. Quinn scoffs, ordering an even larger stack of pancakes with chocolate syrup *and* strawberries on top. I can't help but tease him.

"Quinn…" I sigh with a mock roll of my eyes. "That was my order when I was about eight years old." I give him my best *nanny is judging you* look.

"I don't ignore the little luxuries." He snaps the menu closed with a flourish, and the waiter scoops it up and hurries off with our orders. "Besides, it's what my mother always made. The premixed version with slightly expired chocolate chips, of course, but still. . .it holds memories."

When his eyes crinkle with a softness reserved for his family, I wish, *I want that softness, too,* before I can censor my thoughts.

"Tell me about an average morning for the Kingsley family." Remembering the hard times he and his brothers endured protecting their mother, I quickly clarify. "The *best* kind."

Quinn raises his eyebrows at the request but doesn't object, launching into a story about the time he and his brothers tried to surprise their mother after a particularly difficult night. The result was a mess of their kitchen, a burned batch of chocolate chip cookies, and their poor mother waking to the sound of the smoke alarm. His smile broadens as he describes how angry she was at them for using the oven without her, but how she still ate every bite of their burned surprise.

"I love when you talk about your family," I say at the end of the story, then immediately shove a huge forkful of pancake in my mouth.

He smiles at my enthusiasm, chewing thoughtfully on his first bite. "I just wish I knew more about my mother's family. She cut all ties with them after she got pregnant, and then when our father left her, the bridges were already burned. I was too young to have the foresight to ask her about any other family members. And then she was gone."

I sense the soreness of the topic as he sets his fork down for a moment, briefly having lost his appetite. I reach across the table and grasp his hand firmly.

"You know," I say tentatively, "I had a friend in high school who was adopted. When she turned sixteen, she asked her adoptive parents for one gift—to hire a private investigator to find her birth mother. Awkward family drama aside, it actually worked out well. The PI found her. She posts pictures of them seeing shows together in the city all the time. Crazy, right?" I realize I'm rambling because I'm not sure where this story is going.

"Are you recommending I hire a private

investigator?"

"If you're that curious, you could, yeah," I say, hopeful. "I know it sounds crazy, but it might give you and your brothers some necessary clarity."

Quinn does that thing then, when he squints his eyes and stares at me like I'm an Italian word he's trying to remember but can't quite place.

"I've always had this weight," he admits, and I can tell the words he uses are carefully chosen. "I never considered the possibility of alleviating it. I just thought it was an unanswered question I'd have to live with. Hell," he laughs, "I hire private investigators to track down our runaway clients on almost a weekly basis."

"Maybe it's time to wed professional with personal?" I ask, running my fingers across his knuckles.

"We have gotten pretty good at that, haven't we?" he says with a wink.

I blush, remembering for the first time in days that I'm still his tutor. Professional and personal are lines we've been dancing between since the very beginning. "*Sì*, we certainly have."

Giving him my most innocent smile, I snatch up one of his chocolate-covered strawberries and pop it into my mouth. The flavor is almost as sweet as the word *we* was on my tongue. How incredible is it that such a word can mean so much?

How incredible, and how scary.

Chapter Twelve

Quinn

The crisp morning breeze rushes across my face as I stand on the corner outside my apartment, preparing for my morning jog. As I stretch, I notice that I feel a little lighter than usual. *Probably from all the mind-blowing sex this weekend.* Sex with Alessandra was incredible. Even more incredible than what I've been imagining it would be like for the past couple of weeks.

Once my legs feel loose, I set out at my usual pace, my muscles protesting slightly more than they usually do. I skipped yesterday's jog in favor of breakfast with Alessandra. . .along with a few other unplanned aerobic-like activities.

I forgot how loose a long night of fucking can make you.

Turning the corner at the end of the block, I reach the entrance to my favorite place to jog—a long, looping pathway that winds through the park closest to my apartment. I pick up the pace a bit once my feet hit the dirt. I run this path enough to know that there will be almost no one on it, and I don't have to be as cautious as I do when jogging through the city.

As I make my way down the path, my thoughts wander to my plans for the day. It's Sunday—which means I have family dinner to worry about. It's always good to spend time with my brothers and their wives, but I can already tell I'll struggle to get Alessandra off my mind. After how well she handled the last family dinner, I make a snap decision and pull out my phone.

I slow to a stop in the middle of the pathway and type Alessandra a new message.

Busy tonight? Would love for you to join us for another family dinner.

Moments after I close my phone, it buzzes. A smile spreads across my lips. Good to know Alessandra isn't the type to play hard to get after finally going all the way.

Can't :(Lorraine is out of town, so I have to watch the kids overnight. Wish I could come.

I immediately begin typing a dirty response about coming, but decide against it. Instead, I send:

If I get rid of my family early, can I come see you?

Alessandra responds that she needs to check with her boss first. While waiting for her reply, I begin jogging again.

My phone buzzes, and I quickly stop to open it. I smile as I read the message.

She said it's fine, just as long as it's not too late! Bedtime is 8:30 here. Can't wait to see you. :)

Excited, I send Alessandra a quick text back and practically sprint the rest of the way home. I still have plenty of time to kill before dinner with my family, but knowing that I have time with Alessandra on the horizon gives me a sense of urgency I didn't have before.

The rest of the day catching up on a bit of work, and then cleaning up around the house and prepping for dinner that night. I decide to make sheet-pan fajitas so cleanup will be easy, and I can push my family out the door as soon as we finish with our weekly ritual. I make a quick run to the grocery store to pick up tortillas, then stop by a toy store on the way home to ensure I make a good impression on the kids later.

By the time my brothers arrive with their wives, I can feel myself rushing through our conversations. I have to force myself to listen while Emma and Gavin talk about the renovations to their place, all the while pushing thoughts of Alessandra out of my head.

"You have somewhere to be?" Cooper asks me when Gavin and the women leave the room to set the table. He claps his hand on my shoulder and gives it a good shake. "You haven't stopped checking the clock since the second we got here."

"I, uh, what? No, I'm fine. We have all the time in the world," I mumble, checking on the fajitas in the oven so I don't have to look my brother in the eye.

"Yeah, sure, whatever you say, boss," Cooper grumbles, lazily swirling the wine in his glass. When I don't respond, he decides to press further. "So, where's your girlfriend this fine evening? Did we scare her away?"

I bristle slightly at the word *girlfriend*, not because of what it implies but because I know what Cooper means by it. He's pushing my buttons, and whether I want to admit it or not, it's working.

"She's at work," I say as I pull the fajitas out of the oven.

I check the clock and my stomach sinks a little. It's already seven o'clock. Time to get this show on the road.

"Food's ready," I say loud enough so the others will hear. I decide to help the process along by plating everyone's meals and setting them on the counter for them to grab and go.

"Full service." Emma chuckles, raising her eyebrows as she grabs a plate.

"Yeah, thanks, Quinn," Corinne chimes in, smiling broadly at me.

My brothers and I shuffle into a line behind the women, picking up our plates and making our way to the dining room. Once we're all seated, I make a hasty toast about family time and focus on finishing my meal as soon as possible.

"Have you been fasting all day or something?" Gavin asks, shooting me an amused look.

"I think he's just enjoying his fajitas," Emma says, poking Gavin's ribs with her elbow. "It's delicious,

Quinn."

"Yeah, thanks, Quinn," everyone chimes in before resuming the usual chatter.

While my family continues their conversation about countertops and flooring, I go back and forth between monitoring the time and everyone else's plates. I made sure to only prepare enough food for each person to have one plate, carefully divvying out each meal so there wouldn't be room for seconds. Once everyone finishes eating, I quickly clear all the plates, apologizing for forgetting about dessert.

Slowly, everyone mills into the kitchen to help with cleanup, and by seven-thirty, the place is spotless. As we all stand around the island, chatting casually, I use a natural lull in the conversation to seize my moment.

"Guys, it's been a pleasure, as always," I say, clasping my hands together and forcing a warm smile.

My brothers and sisters-in-law all turn and smile at me, seemingly not understanding that I'm trying to get them to leave.

"Can't wait to do this again next week." I grin even

wider and take a few small steps toward the door.

Gavin furrows his brow, and he and Cooper exchange a slightly annoyed look.

Thankfully, Emma sees the look passed between my brothers and swoops in to save the day. "Well, Quinn, why don't we get out of your hair. Dinner was lovely. Thanks again," she says, looping her arm through Gavin's and pulling him gently toward the door.

Corinne follows suit, thanking me for dinner and taking Cooper's hand in hers.

Thank God for my sisters-in-law, the saviors of my fucking day.

I follow my guests to the front door, wishing them well and assuring them next week's meal will be even tastier. My brothers both shoot me one last disapproving look before leaving, but I'm too distracted to care. It's already seven-forty, and when I looked up directions to Lorraine's house earlier in the day, my phone said it would take about twenty minutes to get there.

I quickly brush my teeth to eliminate any trace of fajita breath, grab the bag with the toys for the kids, and get into my car. During the drive to Lorraine's house, that stupid butterfly feeling flutters in my stomach again. This isn't the first time it's happened, but still, I can't help but feel a little embarrassed.

I'm thirty-fucking-eight years old. So, why the hell do I suddenly feel twenty-three all over again?

By the time I pull up in front of the house, the light rain that started halfway through my drive has escalated just short of a downpour. I check the clock for the last time. Eight o'clock. Only half an hour before bedtime, but hey, at least I made it.

The nerves haven't really died down in my stomach, but at this point, I'm more concerned about the growing bulge in my pants. Just thinking about Alessandra brings me right back to the feeling of her velvety skin, the image of her perfect body writhing in pleasure. I run my hands roughly over my face before getting out of the car.

I need to focus. I'm meeting the kids she babysits, for fuck's sake. This isn't the time to arrive at her doorstep with a fucking hard-on.

Stepping out into the rain-soaked street and before I

take off running for the front door, I take the bag in one hand, quickly locking the car behind me with the other. In the fifteen seconds it takes me to jog from the curb to the door, I wish I'd thought to bring flowers for Alessandra—and an umbrella for me. *Too late now, asshole.* Hopefully, she finds the slightly damp look endearing.

After three solid knocks, I take a step back and wait for the door to open. I can hear a squeal from the other side of the door, and a child's voice screaming something I can't really make out.

Within moments, the door swings open and Alessandra is standing in front of me. I haven't seen her since breakfast yesterday morning. Even though I know she must be exhausted from watching her little monsters all day, I can't tell from her face. She's as radiant and gorgeous as always, somehow still sexy in an oversized gray sweatshirt and leggings.

She smiles at me, and for a moment, neither of us says anything. I can almost hear the energy crackling between us, and already I know—this is gonna be one hell of an evening.

Chapter Thirteen

Alessandra

"Erica, can you say hi to Quinn?"

Staring out at Quinn Kingsley on the porch—his navy blazer speckled with rain drops, that perfect half smile on his lips—I feel as though I'm looking into a dream. It hardly feels real that he would wrap up dinner with his family early in favor of keeping me company while I'm watching the munchkins. But here he is, as real as ever, carrying a reusable grocery bag in his arms.

Trading in her usual sass for shyness, Erica peeks her head out from behind me and smiles bashfully before hiding again, her white-blonde hair falling in front of her eyes. It's unlike her to be this way, but then again, I can't blame her. I was taken aback the first time I met Quinn, too.

I remember that flustered version of myself who was shocked at her own ability to be flirtatious with a man who was so intense, so easy to get lost in. That was only a couple of weeks ago, but it seems like much longer with everything that's happened.

"Aren't you gonna let him in before he gets all rained on?" Shy Erica has disappeared, and Sassy Erica makes her return.

Have I been staring long? My cheeks are warm as I step out of the doorway to let Quinn inside. He squeezes my ass as he walks by and I can't muffle my gasp, but Erica has already booked it back to the family room, thank God. She's trying to hold Ben in her small, clumsy arms, obviously showing off for our guest. Again, I totally can't blame her.

Quinn sets the grocery bag on the kitchen counter and rustles through it for a moment before emerging with a princess doll and a toy fire truck.

"It seems like you have quite a few toys already," he says, surveying the family room floor, which looks like a Toys"R"Us exploded. "I hope you don't mind if I add a few more to your collection."

Erica locks eyes with the doll from across the room, and her face lights up like it's Christmas morning. She sets Ben back down on his play mat and races toward Quinn, grabbing for her new toy.

"What do you think, will she do?" Quinn says in a kid-friendly voice that I've never heard him use before. It's lighter, softer, more relaxed than his usual intense tone.

He hands the doll to Erica, who giggles, running her fingers over the pink terrycloth onesie the doll is wearing. She's one of those dolls that looks like a real baby, and Erica is enamored. I used to have a doll like that as a girl, and can still remember the baby-powder scent of her rubbery skin.

Ben, who has crawled into the kitchen, lets out an excited squeal and tugs on Quinn's pants leg.

"It's all yours, little guy." Quinn squats down to meet Ben at eye level and gives the truck a light push across the kitchen tile. Ben claps his tiny hands together and chases after it.

"Don't worry, I brought presents for you, too," Quinn calls back to me as the three of them make their way to Ben's play mat, stepping over carefully built block castles and stuffed-animal tea parties.

I peek into the grocery bag—a plastic container of

chicken fajitas and a bottle of pinot noir. I glance at him from across the room, and he gives me a wink.

Am I imagining this? My plan for the evening was to force down the leftover frozen pizza after I put the kids to bed, then maybe text Quinn, fully knowing he might not respond until after his family heads home. My idea of company for the night was whoever was hosting the late-night talk shows. This seems like an alternate reality I could only have dreamed up.

I put the food in the fridge and join the three amigos in the living room, where Quinn has found himself on the bottom of a three-person dog pile. I can't help but laugh, and none of us stop laughing for the next half hour of playtime.

It almost physically pains me when I have to announce that it's bedtime. Actually, bedtime was about ten minutes ago, but I didn't have the heart to stop the kids from playing with their new toys and their new best friend. Luckily, all the playing horsey and wrestling has worn Erica out enough that she only whines a little about having to call it a night.

"Can he come back and play next time?" she pleads,

grabbing Quinn's hand.

"Maybe, we'll see," I say, figuring that *no, your new best friend has to work his job at his high-profile escort service* isn't the best answer for a six-year-old. What she doesn't know won't hurt her. "C'mon, say good-bye to Quinn so we can go get your jammies on."

Erica squeezes Quinn into a quick hug before taking off to her room. *How does she have any energy left?* Meanwhile, Ben is out like a light on his play mat.

"How can I help?" Quinn says, as if he hasn't helped enough already. Ben has never fallen asleep so easily, and there are faint sounds of the faucet running and Erica brushing her teeth upstairs, which never happens without several bribes first.

I can't help myself—I grab the lapel of Quinn's blazer and pull him in for the slow, warm kiss I've been waiting to give since I opened that door.

"I can take it from here," I whisper, squeezing his shoulder and giving him one last peck on the cheek. He shakes his head and smiles, scooping up Ben and laying him in my arms as if he's done it a thousand times before.

"Ti aspetterò," he says. *I'll be waiting for you.*

I carry Ben upstairs and into the nursery. After changing his diaper and dressing him in his jammies, I carefully lay him in his crib.

Erica has toothpaste all over her pink nightgown, but her teeth are brushed and she's yawning after I read her only half a princess story, so I call it an overall victory. The story is one I've read aloud to her at least a dozen times, a standard fairy tale about a handsome prince who falls in love with a princess, but with Quinn waiting for me downstairs, I'm buying into the fantasy a little more than I usually do. As Erica nods off, I promise we'll finish the story in the morning.

Once the lights are out and the blankets are tucked in, I descend the stairs to my own personal Prince Charming, who has already heated up my dinner and poured us each a generous glass of wine while he sits on the sofa, awaiting my return. He's ditched his blazer, and the sleeves of his button-down shirt are pushed up to his elbows. God, does he have any idea how sexy that is?

I nestle in next to him on the couch and he drapes an arm around me, pulling me in tight against him. I press my lips gently to his cheek, then smile as my lips meet his. Quinn lets out a slow exhale of pleasure, followed by a quiet laugh.

"You should eat. Playing with them burns an unbelievable amount of energy," he teases, motioning to the plate on the coffee table.

I pull away, disappointed to have been cut off. Still, as much as I'd rather be tasting him, I can't deny that I'm starving. I take a long, much-deserved sip of wine.

"Thank you for all of this—the toys, the playtime, the food." I take a bite of chicken fajita, which tastes less like leftovers and more like a miracle. It's almost impossible to believe that for all of his many talents, he also cooks, too. Between the cooking and the kids, I'm starting to believe there's nothing Quinn Kingsley can't do.

"You're very welcome."

Between bites, I tell Quinn about my day with the kids, which he seems to enjoy even more now that he's met them. In turn, he tells me about dinner with his family.

"We all missed having you," he says, and I shyly push a red pepper slice across the plate with my fork. The thought of his family discussing me at dinner simultaneously thrills me and makes my palms sweat.

"It's getting late. I suppose I should let you get some rest," he says, glancing at his watch. "If I'm tired from half an hour with the kids, I imagine you must be ready to crash."

My stomach drops at the mention of him leaving.

"Can you stay just a tiny bit longer?" I smile up at him. "You've been wonderful tonight. I can't let you leave without thanking you."

"Oh?" His forehead wrinkles as he lifts one inquisitive brow. "What did you have in mind?"

"Be right back."

I place my dish and the empty wineglasses on the kitchen counter. Then I take Quinn's hand and lead him from the couch, through the maze of toys and down the hall to the room that I'll be calling home for the night. It's Lorraine's craft room, but in addition to the sewing machine and desk, there's a futon that she's folded out into a bed for me, complete with clean white sheets.

I reach for the doorknob, pressing my finger to my lips as a reminder that we'll have to keep this quiet. Quinn nods, following so close behind me that I can feel the bulge in his pants brush against the small of my back, which makes every muscle in my body clench. It's a wonder I've kept my hands to myself this long.

He glances around the room as I close the door behind us. The mood is already set with the soft glow of a lamp.

Carefully, I drop to my knees before him, and meet his eyes which are growing darker with his desire.

"Alessandra?" he asks.

I don't think I'll ever grow tired of my name on his lips, or the way his deep baritone rolls over the word.

Chapter Fourteen

Quinn

Heaven. This is heaven.

With Alessandra's mouth around my cock, I could dissolve into a damn puddle right here on the carpeting. She's fucking amazing.

"Shit, yes. Just like that." I smooth her hair back from her face, watching her work over my cock like it's her own personal lollipop. "So damn good, sweetheart."

She pulls away for a moment, eyes heated with lust I haven't seen in her eyes before. Breathily, she responds. "I love doing this for you, Quinn."

Fuck. That only makes it hotter. "God, baby, yes, suck me."

"Mmm," she hums around me as she licks and laves my shaft. "You like that?"

Of course, I fucking do. "I think you know the answer to that," I say on a groan. "Don't you dare stop."

My little beauty grins up at me with my cock in her

mouth. I almost come on the spot.

With that mind-numbing fantasy playing out in front of me, the desire to come for her, to give myself to her, wins out over everything else. I grip her hair, pleasure rippling through me in waves as I grip her head and give myself to her as deep as she can take me. "Yes, yes, yes."

Alessandra responds perfectly—as I knew she would. As she swallows my whole length down her throat, I can't help but be amazed.

My God, who is this woman? How long can I continue to tell myself that she's merely my Italian tutor?

She's quickly becoming so much more.

Cradling Alessandra's cheek with one hand, I guide her mouth to mine in a thankful kiss. As our tongues meet, the slight salty taste only reminds me just how perfect and sexy she is. Wrapping my arms around her, I lay Alessandra down on the pull-out mattress, already hungry to taste her, too.

I move my lips to her neck, my fingers slipping under the waistband of her tight little leggings. She moans softly at my touch, and suddenly all I want is for her to make more sounds like that.

Peeling her leggings away, I take a moment to appreciate how she looks all laid out, waiting for what I'm about to do with her. "I want to taste you."

Alessandra smiles but says nothing. Instead, she places her index finger over her lips, reminding me that we must be quiet.

Good luck with that, sweetheart. I remove her lacy panties and descend upon her needy core, relishing the way her hips move in response to my tongue.

"Oh, my God." She whimpers, arching her back, her breathing more labored than before.

Using one hand to steady her hips, I raise my other hand to her breast, massaging it gently and teasing her nipple between my fingers. After how good she made me feel, I want to do everything I can to return the favor.

When I give her nipple a small pinch, Alessandra responds with another moan, just like I hoped. I slip my tongue inside her, running my thumb over her swollen bud, loving every reaction I coax from her.

I continue working my tongue over her, lapping her

up until she comes, turning and burying her face into her pillow to muffle her moans.

As her breathing slows and her body relaxes, I lie next to her and wrap her soft, supple body in my arms. She curls into me, placing her head on my chest and tracing tiny circles on my skin with her fingers.

"Thank you," she whispers.

"You don't have to thank me," I whisper back, wrapping my arms tighter around her. We lie there for a while, trading soft murmurs, until I feel Alessandra's body grow heavy with sleep.

"Okay, I should head home," I whisper, and place a soft kiss on her brow.

"Nooo." She groans, sliding closer into me and wrapping a leg around my waist.

"It's getting late." I chuckle, reluctantly pulling her leg away from me. "And I don't want you getting in trouble."

"I guess you're right." She sighs, slowly unraveling herself from my arms.

I get up from the bed and begin putting my clothes back on. Alessandra sits up, a small pout on her pretty lips.

"Or you could stay for just a little while longer," she says, her eyes sad.

"You're tired. You need to get some rest. And something tells me if I stay, sleep is the last thing that'll happen."

She smiles, her gaze flitting over to her panties in the corner of the room. "I don't know what you're talking about," she says softly, stretching her arms in the air, putting her perfect tits on full display.

"That is exactly what I'm talking about." I smile. *Such a sexy little minx.* "I'll text you in the morning, okay?"

She nods and rises from the bed, and we straighten our clothes.

Once I'm dressed, the two of us tiptoe to the front door, where I kiss her softly before she closes the door gently behind me.

As I drive home, thoughts of Alessandra swirl through my mind.

When she answered the front door wearing those black leggings and a white T-shirt tied at the waist? *Fuck me.* This evening was a foregone conclusion. She looked like every coed fantasy I've ever had come to life.

While driving over here, after kicking my entire family out of my apartment, I honestly thought *'What in the fuck am I doing? Going to some lady's house where my barely legal girlfriend works as a nanny? Creeper alert! Fuck off, Quinn. Turn around and go home.'* But of course, I didn't.

And when I arrived and Alessandra was so nervous and gracious, and also surprised that I actually showed up—I couldn't help it. I became legitimately excited, and I went all in. I felt inspired enough to play with the children, right there on the living room floor. Shit, and when had kids been so giggly? I can't remember another time I felt like that. And the warm smile on Alessandra's face as she watched was worth all of that and more.

When I get home to my empty house, it feels quieter, colder than it ever did before. All at once, it finally hits me how alone I was before Alessandra came along. Before she was a part of my life, I never thought I'd be the kind of man to crawl around on the floor with small children.

And now? I can't wait to do it again.

Just as the warmth of my feelings for Alessandra settle in, I remember that she's leaving, and it hits me like a ton of bricks.

I miss her already, after lying next to her only twenty minutes ago. How will I handle it when she's an ocean away?

Seeing her tonight with the kids. . .she was so cute and funny. It was a side of her I've never seen before, and it brought out a side of me I didn't know I had. Every time I'm with her, I learn something new. About me, about her, about us.

This whole time, I've been trying to convince myself that this thing between us is a short-lived fling, even in the moments when part of me feels like it's something more. I know she's probably all wrong for me. I know that the age difference makes it complicated. But in this moment, here in my cold, empty apartment, I realize something that changes everything—I don't fucking care about all that anymore.

I don't care if she's all wrong for me. I don't care if she's too young. I don't care if she's moving across the world and leaving me behind.

I'm going all in. And I don't think there's anything I can do now to stop it.

Chapter Fifteen

Alessandra

Erica's tiny arms are wrapped tightly around my hips in a way that is both endearing and cutting off my circulation. I finally broke it to my favorite little brats about a week ago that I won't be around to clean up their spilled juice boxes much longer, and the imminent threat of me leaving has Erica acting uncharacteristically affectionate. Ben, who is currently resting on his mom's hip as she scribbles out my check, is too young to be fazed. I'm sort of jealous of him that he doesn't have to deal with good-byes.

"No, you're stuck with me for a few more days," I say, shaking the grip of Erica's Play-Doh-covered hands. Maybe I should have broken the news sooner and enjoyed a few more weeks of this. It sure beats the usual symphony of screams and constant sass over the injustice of me suggesting she eat a vegetable.

"I wish you could stay forever!" She sticks out her bottom lip, batting her big brown eyes at me.

"Erica, no pouting," Lorraine snaps, ripping my check out of her checkbook and handing it to me. She's been especially quick-tempered with the kids lately, probably because of the stress of trying to find a replacement nanny. "Thank you so much, Alessandra, and I'm sorry I was late. Again."

I check the time on my phone—she was forty-five minutes late tonight, and this is becoming a new habit for her.

"Don't stress it at all," I say, and I actually mean it. I guess getting laid really does put people in a better mood. I fold the check in half and slip it into my purse as I head toward the door.

"*Ciao*, Erica. *Ciao*, Ben."

"*Ciao*, Alessandra!" Erica shouts. This is the first time she's repeated any Italian back to me.

I want to turn around and hug her, but I can't stick around for what would undoubtedly be another twenty-minute ordeal of Erica attaching herself to me. I have dinner plans with Deanna at a sushi spot we've been meaning to hit up since it opened two months ago, one more item on the list of things we have to do together before I leave. Once I'm on the train, I shoot her a text to give her a heads-up on my late arrival, then immediately draft a flirty text to Quinn.

The past week has been an incredibly delicate balancing act of my work, social, and sex lives in an attempt to get in the best of everything before I go. It's been the perfect kind of hectic. The kind where I'm gossiping with Deanna over a bottle of wine one hour, and whispering dirty Italian and nibbling on Quinn's ear the next.

The restaurant is two blocks away from my train stop, allowing me enough time on my walk over to swipe a coat of gloss across my lips and check my hair in the front-facing camera on my phone. I look surprisingly put together for a girl who spent the day cleaning spaghetti sauce off the face of a one-year-old. My hair has held its loose curls, and the first breezes of early fall have left my cheeks the perfect amount of rosy. I walk into the dimly lit restaurant feeling like I was plucked from the pages of *Vogue* instead of having just gotten off a hot, overcrowded train car.

Deanna is already settled in at a table, sipping a glass

of wine and perusing the menu. When I sit down, she motions for the waitress to bring another glass for me.

"Okay, you look way too good for having wrangled kids all day. Are you meeting Quinn after this or something?"

She's right to be suspicious. It wouldn't be the first time I've gone straight to Quinn's place after plans with her. One of the items on the infinitely long list of reasons I love Deanna is that she's never gotten jealous about a guy, and Quinn has been no exception. Still, we only have a matter of days left to get in the last of our Aly-and-Deanna time, so I told Quinn tonight was a no-go.

"Nope. Tonight it's just you, me, and as many spicy tuna rolls as we can handle."

We order a first round of sushi to split, and in the quietest voice I can manage, I fill Deanna in on my tryst with Quinn last night. I keep the details to a minimum for the sake of the waitress, who arrives with a platter of sushi as I'm wrapping up my story.

"All while the kids were asleep upstairs. Damn, Aly. I didn't know you had it in you."

Deanna picks up a piece of sushi with her chopsticks and brings it slowly and suggestively between her lips, letting out a low hum of satisfaction. I do my best to stifle my giggles.

"You should've seen how good he was with the kids. I couldn't help myself."

My mind wanders back to watching Quinn push the wooden truck across the rug with Ben as Erica clung like a monkey to his back, vying for his attention. "I can't believe I'm saying it, Deanna, but I think I'm falling for him."

She nods, seemingly unsurprised. "So, what are you going to do, then? Swap out that plane ticket on your vision board for a picture of his face?"

The idea of staying in Boston to be with Quinn crosses my mind at least a dozen times a day. I have more than enough money saved for a plane ticket home if I still want to spend a few weeks in Italy. Maybe Quinn would even want to come with me. I can imagine sipping coffee with him on the cobblestone streets of Rome, clinging to his perfectly toned arms as we hike the cliffs on the Amalfi Coast.

Every hair on my arms stands on end as I snap out of my fantasy.

Italy with Quinn would be a daydream come true, but then what? I come home and keep being a nanny? Tutoring here in Boston is decent money, but certainly not enough to live off of. How can I abandon my dream at the last second? But then again, how can I leave Quinn behind just as I'm beginning to fall for him?

Whenever I'm stuck, I always imagine what I would say if Deanna were in my shoes. What advice would I give her? Without a second thought, I would tell her to get on that plane.

"I have to go to Italy. It's non-negotiable at this point." I pop a piece of California roll into my mouth to give myself time to actually believe what I just said. "He hasn't even mentioned the idea of me staying. Plus, what am I supposed to do. . .ditch my dream, stay here and remain a nanny, just for a chance with Quinn?" My voice trembles a bit as I say his name, my toes curling inside my boots, but I have to be practical. Quinn is a maybe, but Italy is a guarantee.

"You're right," Deanna says, and I'm half surprised

to hear it from her. "Besides, you haven't even known him that long. You have no idea if you guys would work out."

"Exactly. We could date for a year and be happy, but then what? There are no guarantees. What if it runs its course? I would never forgive myself for bailing on Italy for a man." *Even for a man as perfect as Quinn.*

Deanna forces her mouth into a half smile. As much as she has been my cheerleader throughout the process of deciding to make the move to the other side of the ocean, I know it's hurting her as my departure gets closer and closer. It's a lot easier to tell your best friend to follow her dreams than to watch her actually board the plane.

"And who knows, I probably won't stay in Italy forever," I remind her. "Maybe he'll still be single when I come back. If it's meant to be, it's meant to be."

This loosens Deanna up a little bit. She lifts her half-empty glass of pinot grigio in the air, and I follow suit.

"To following your dreams," she says, "and to hoping they lead you back to living on the same continent as me someday."

Clink.

Chapter Sixteen

Quinn

I swear to God, I would give just about anything to be able to stop time, just for this week.

Alessandra leaves me in four days. It's been business as usual lately, all our girls showing up on time, all our clients paying in a timely manner. But even while business is booming and my brothers are in high spirits, I can't shake the uneasy feeling creeping over me the closer Alessandra's departure date becomes.

For the first time in my life, I feel helpless. What can I possibly do? Ask her to change her mind? And for what. . .to stay in Boston and be a nanny? Italy is her passion, the dream she's held on to for as long as she can remember. What kind of man would I be if I asked her to give that up?

I promised myself a few days ago to let her go. To make the most of this last week with her and take her departure like a man. There are certain things I just can't offer her. The dream life she's planned for herself in Italy is one of them. So, for now, all that's left for me to do is make her remaining time here as magical and painless as possible. And that starts with an incredible dinner—and ends with mind-blowing sex.

Just as I pull out my phone to text her and confirm our dinner plans later, a ping draws my attention to my computer where a new email notification has popped up. At first, I don't recognize the address. I put my phone back down on my desk and frown at the screen as I click open the email, and the first line makes my heart skip a beat.

Mr. Kingsley—Found information regarding your mother's family. Call for details.

I read the email, then read it again, my eyes moving so quickly that the words blur together. When I hired a private investigator after Alessandra suggested it, I didn't think anything would come of it. I've heard so many stories about these guys being major scams, half of me is screaming that this is just another lie, another asshole out to make a buck off my sentimental curiosity.

But the other half of me needs to know exactly what

this asshole thinks he found.

I pick up my phone and immediately dial the PI's number, my heart racing five times faster than it was a second ago. The phone rings longer than I expected, and just as I'm about to hang up, throwing away the possibility of a larger family, I'm stopped by a gruff, scratchy voice.

"Yeah, all right, what is it?"

I roll my eyes. Why does this guy have to be such a fucking stereotype? "This is Quinn Kingsley. I just got your email."

He clears his throat. "Right, Mr. Kingsley. You might want to sit down for this."

"Already got that covered, thanks." *Just spit it out, already.*

"Well, I ran your mother's name through some different databases, and, uh, it looks like she gave up a baby for adoption about thirty-six years ago. A boy. I found the guy's address if you're interested."

The investigator keeps talking but I tune him out, my mind suddenly fuzzy and blank. A baby?

What the fuck is going on?

"Listen, I don't know what you think you found," I say, cutting him off, "but that's impossible. I have two brothers, and there's no way our mother would have kept a fourth one from us."

"I only found a first name," he says, ignoring my comments. "It's, uh. . .William. He's thirty-seven and lives in a suburb outside the city."

Thirty-seven. That puts him right between me and Gavin.

Holy fucking shit.

I quickly wrap up the conversation with the PI, who doesn't have any more information to offer. He tells me the bill should arrive in the mail this week, and I tell him I'll pay him extra if he can find me a way to contact this guy. Phone number, home address, email. . .hell, at this point I'll take carrier pigeon.

When I hang up the phone, I'm still reeling from the news. Another brother. After all these years…

Suddenly, Cooper comes bursting through my office door, a large stack of folders in his hands, already explaining what forms I need to sign. But the moment he sees the shock plastered on my face, he replaces his serious business tone with a sly, mocking one.

"What, did your nineteen-year-old girlfriend dump you or something? Was it a problem with her bedtime?"

I don't answer, instead burying my face in my hands, my elbows propped on my desk.

"Hey, look, man, I'm sorry. I know she's twenty-two; I'm just busting your balls. Breakups are, uh, hard. Trust me, if anyone understands, it's me."

Cooper's words barely register with me. I still can't believe that we have another brother.

"Seriously, dude, what's going on?" He sets the folders down on the edge of my desk.

I run my hands roughly over my face before sighing and looking my brother in the eye. "You might want to sit down."

He sits, and I explain to him what I just learned from the private investigator. After Cooper's initial shock wears off, we agree to set this information aside for now and tell Gavin together when he gets back from a work trip to

Florida.

As Cooper stands to leave, he shakes his head and chuckles. "I seriously thought when I first walked in that something had happened with Alessandra."

"Yeah, well. That's a whole other issue. This is her last week in America."

"Fuck, dude. Better make the most of it."

• • •

The rest of the week flies by in a blur. Alessandra and I spend every free moment we have together, grabbing a delicious bite to eat and making love with more urgency and passion than ever before. I've had a hard time focusing on work all week—Alessandra has picked up the habit of sending me dirty texts in Italian, just in case anyone catches a glimpse of one of our messages.

Earlier in the week, Alessandra had to cancel our hastily scheduled quickie to babysit the kids for an extra half hour. Apparently, Lorraine got stuck in traffic, and even though the kids were asleep, someone had to be there to watch them. We would have moved our quickie to later, but I had a work function to attend that my brothers couldn't cover, so Alessandra and I resolved to spend that half hour on the phone, laughing and chatting and doing everything in our power to pretend our relationship wouldn't be ending in a matter of days.

Now the week is almost over. She's leaving tomorrow, and I haven't seen her all day. Deanna planned a small get-together for Alessandra tonight, and even though she invited me, I decided it would be best if I let her friends have her for the night. Lord knows we'd never be able to keep our eyes—or our hands—off each other.

I decide to send Alessandra one last dirty text for the night, just to tide her over until our last date before she leaves tomorrow evening.

You can't imagine what I will do to you later.

She responds: *I have some ideas.*

I spend the rest of the night finishing as much work as I can so that my time with Alessandra tomorrow can be as long and meaningful as possible. But in the back of my mind throughout the rest of my night, I can't do anything to silence the small, panicked voice in the back of my mind saying, *What the hell am I gonna do when the woman I love leaves?*

• • •

Alessandra knocks on my door at three. As I make my way from the living room to greet her, I go over the timeline before she leaves in my head. It's three o'clock now. Her flight leaves at eight. She needs to be at the airport at five-thirty. She needs to leave my place at five. We have two hours.

Two fucking hours. Before she's out of my life forever.

I open the door to find Alessandra standing there in gray leggings and a dark blue oversized sweater, her two jam-packed suitcases on either side of her. She gives me a small smile, and I can feel us both straining to pretend that everything's fine.

"Let me take those," I say, stepping forward to drag her suitcases inside.

"*Grazie,*" she murmurs, moving aside so I can take them.

Once her bags are inside and out of the way, I usher Alessandra in and place a soft kiss on her cheek. "*Prego.*"

She responds to my kiss by wrapping her arms around me, pulling me in for a long, warm embrace. As the two of us stand there holding each other, it takes every ounce of strength in me not to tell her to blow off her flight, to just stay here in my arms forever.

When we pull back, I brush her hair out of her eyes, holding her cheek in my palm. *"Mio bellissimo,"* I whisper. *My beautiful.*

Alessandra turns and presses a kiss into my hand before stepping away from me and sighing. "If we start our sappy good-byes now, I'll be too exhausted to get on that plane later," she says with a chuckle.

She's joking, I know, but part of me really can't resist…

"Is that a promise?"

I step forward to close the distance between us, slipping my hand around her waist and pulling her hips against mine. I know it's not fair, I know I'm playing dirty, but every fiber of my being is telling me to make her stay. The voice in the back of my head is screaming, *Fight, motherfucker, fight!*

"Quinn…" Alessandra stops and turns her face to avoid my eyes as she pulls away.

"I know, I know," I mutter, releasing her from my arms and stepping back. "I'm only teasing. You'll love Italy." *Stupid, Kingsley, stupid.*

Alessandra smiles and says nothing, running her fingers through her hair. I can't tell if it's just me, but I think she's avoiding eye contact.

"Can I get you anything?" I turn toward the kitchen and motion for her to follow. "Water, seltzer, glass of wine? I have food, as well, if you're hungry. . .cheese, crackers, popcorn, grapes, whatever your heart desires."

"A glass of water would be great," she says, her voice a little too high.

As I fill two glasses of water, she sits on the couch, her gaze wandering over the room like she's trying to soak up every detail. When I join her, I ask about the get-together with Deanna last night, and we quickly begin chatting with ease again. I do my best to focus as she explains the crazy cocktails Deanna made her drink, but I find myself compulsively checking the time, wishing desperately that it would slow down—or even stop—just this once.

When the clock strikes four-thirty, I shift in my seat, waiting for her to pause so I can seize the moment. She's been talking about the travel guides and portable phone chargers her friends gave her as going-away presents, and I figure now is as good a time as any to give her mine.

Alessandra pauses, and when she sees that my expression has changed, she playfully raises an eyebrow. "What's that look?" she asks, a grin spreading across her face.

"Wait right here." I stand and walk over to the kitchen counter, where I've tucked a small box out of sight.

Her playful look fades into one of understanding, and her face falls a little when she sees the small blue box, its white ribbon crisp and shining. "Oh, Quinn, you didn't have to—" she says, but I raise my hand and shake my head to stop her.

"This has nothing to do with obligation." I sit next to her on the couch, closer than before. "I wanted to." When I place the box in her lap, she takes it delicately in her hands, rubbing the edges of the ribbon between her fingers.

"Should I pack this away and open it later?" she asks, reaching for her purse.

"No, please, open it now." I place my hand on her thigh.

"Okay," she says softly, tugging gently on the ends of the ribbon to undo the bow. The ribbon falls away from the box, and I watch her eyes grow wide and watery as she opens the lid, finding the necklace I picked out for her weeks ago.

"Quinn, it's. . .it's beautiful," she says, her voice soft and shaky. She lifts the delicate chain out of the box, holding its pearl pendant at eye level.

"May I?" I ask, reaching out my hand.

She nods, giving me the necklace and turning away from me, sweeping her long, dark hair over her shoulder. I place my gift around her neck, my fingertips brushing against the velvety skin of the nape of her neck as I fasten the tiny clasp.

"How does it look?" she asks, turning to face me

straight on, fluffing her hair around her shoulders.

"*Bellissima.*" I smile. It's perfect on her, just like I knew it would be.

Alessandra leans in and places a small peck on my lips before taking my cheek in her hand and pulling me in for a longer, slower kiss. Our lips begin moving faster and more impatiently, and I move my hands all over her body, taking in every last inch of her before she leaves.

I can feel a bulge growing behind my zipper as I grab a handful of her ass, her soft moan escaping into my mouth. I'm about to pull her on top of me, prepared to let our bodies do what they do so well, when she suddenly pulls away, retreating to the other end of the couch, leaving a good two feet of space between us.

She runs her fingers over the pendant, tears welling in her eyes. "There's not enough time," she murmurs, her breathing ragged.

I nod and clear my throat, shifting to make my erection slightly more concealed and comfortable. Alessandra and I watch each other in silence for a moment, our breathing heavy and labored, until I break the silence with a sigh.

"Are you sure you have to go?" It kills me to ask the question, but it would hurt even more not to try.

She stares at me with wide, glassy eyes, her mouth slightly open. When she blinks, a single tear rolls down her cheek. "Yes, I'm sure." Before I can reach out, she quickly wipes away the tear, then sniffs and clears her throat. "Sal is back working. He'll be your tutor again starting next week."

I nod silently, swallowing the lump rising in my throat.

She glances at the clock on the wall. Four fifty-seven. "I should go," she whispers, rising and slinging her purse over her shoulder.

I walk her to the door, dragging her suitcases out for her. We stand in the open doorway, waiting in silence for her taxi. Within moments, the car arrives, and I carry her suitcases behind her and lift them into the trunk.

I open the car door for her, and she places her carry-on in the backseat. Alessandra turns and throws her arms around me, squeezing me harder than she ever has before.

We kiss briefly, careful to not fall into our passionate rhythm again, before giving each other one last, long look.

"Safe travels," I say, pressing my lips softly against her forehead.

"*Grazie*," she replies, her eyes searching mine. "For everything. Really."

"No, *bellissima*, thank *you*."

She climbs into the backseat and I close the door behind her, stepping back onto the curb as the taxi slowly pulls away, picking up speed as it merges into traffic.

I stand there watching the cab until it fades into a small yellow dot in the distance, turns the corner, and takes Alessandra away and out of my life—forever.

Chapter Seventeen

Alessandra

Staring into the three distinct fingerprints in my personal jar of peanut butter is a rude awakening this morning. I can hear Deanna's reaction in my head, as clear as day. *Your roommate eats your food with her bare hands? What is she, a raccoon? Girl, NO.*

I learned that Flora, my new roommate, has very few boundaries the moment I first opened the door two weeks ago, laden with my luggage. She greeted me from the couch upon which she sprawled, naked from the waist down. A gasp and perhaps a dramatic averting of my eyes didn't move her in the slightest to go put pants on.

Instead, she waved me in, complaining, "Come in, come in. There's a draft."

Good thing I'm fluent in Italian because introductions could have been even worse, if that's possible to imagine. It only got better when I learned of her live-in boyfriend. No need to be fluent in *any* language to recognize the animalistic moaning and growling of their lovemaking in the next room. These walls aren't just thin—they are Vatican-wafer thin, but without any of the decorum.

I stare at the horrible lines in my peanut butter jar, tears threatening to spill out of the corners of my eyes. Deanna gave it to me as a parting gift. *Take this in memory of me, and eat it while you wish you were back in the land of saturated fats,* she said, a smirk on her perfectly painted lips.

Flora must have found it when she came home at five in the morning, drunk and stomping around like a goddamn elephant. Or worse, maybe she found it while sober and simply thought it was fine to scoop it right out of my super-special homesick stash of American snacks.

She's like a child. A small child. Nothing you aren't familiar with. You're good with children, I remind myself. But this bitch is *not* a child. She's a grown woman whom I can't put in time-out for being nasty or rude. I can't imagine Erica behaving this badly, or even little Ben. So here I am, living in the nightmarish reality of a terrible roommate, actually missing the little monsters I used to take care of.

I realize I'm still staring at the polluted jar of peanut butter. With a huff, I jam the lid back on and twist. Into the trash it goes, along with my moronic dreams of how this trip was supposed to begin.

According to my dream vision, I was supposed to live in a moderately sized two-bedroom, with a small living room and a spacious kitchen for all the fantastic dinners I would be making. There would maybe even be a balcony where I would sip my delicious Italian coffee early in the mornings as I watched the sun rise over the stone buildings. My roommate was supposed to be some magic clone of Deanna, who knew all the fun clubs to hit up and coffee shops to contemplate the mysteries of life in. I was supposed to fit right in here, like a lost little puzzle piece of the great Colosseum, finally found.

Instead, I have mildew in the bathroom, barred windows, and a roommate who leaves at midnight to do God knows what and doesn't come back until five in the morning.

I find myself reminiscing. *I miss Ben and his cute little diaper-butt.* The absurdity of the thought makes me laugh out loud. Am I really missing the messes of being a nanny? They were simple. I knew how to calm a tantrum, wipe up a mess, and improvise a game. It may have been exhausting some days, but at least it was familiar. This new life isn't one I know how to navigate.

I open my computer, wrapping my cardigan closely around me. Today is Saturday, finally, and my first free day since landing in Italy. All other days have been filled with back-to-back private tutoring lessons.

The agency has no office, which was a shock. I have yet to meet my supervisor. My only interaction with the agency has been via email. One thing they didn't tell me prior to hiring me is that these would be home visits— homes that I would need a mode of transportation to get to. I couldn't very well bring a car across the ocean with me, and I have yet to find any affordable public transportation. A rickety bike I bought for twenty euros at a pawn shop has brought me from location to location, sometimes only to be greeted by a frown and *"No, grazie. Addio!"* No, thanks, no lesson today. Good-bye! And so back on the bike I go.

With a quick shake of my shoulders, I try to think positively. At least I get paid today. Everything is much more expensive here than I remember from my class trip so many years ago. The past two weeks have consisted of eating half portions of my usual meals just to get through the day without falling over from fatigue and malnutrition. Fresh, bountiful groceries are at the top of my list. My stomach grumbles angrily at me, deprived of my usual breakfast of toast and peanut butter. Yes, food is a top priority.

I access my bank account online to check for the direct deposit of my first paycheck. The Internet connection chugs along at a depressing rate, and I tap my fingers impatiently. It finally opens.

That can't be right. Two hundred euros for two weeks? I do the math quickly in my head. That's under two hundred fifty dollars for all the lessons, uphill pedaling, and doors slammed in my face. I rifle through the papers strewn across my table, looking for my contract. Surely there must be a mistake.

A hundred euros every day of lessons, right? Certainly, that's what it said. I couldn't have misread it. I find the number with a sigh of relief, and now I look for the rate.

Congrua. Stipend. My rate is a *weekly stipend* of one hundred euros.

The tears I forced away after the peanut-butter crisis

return now, full force. I crumple to the floor with a whimper, feeling like an idiot.

How could I have signed this silly piece of paper? How could I have been so blinded by my vision of Italy that I didn't read the fine print? One hundred euros a week is simply not a livable wage. I'll starve in this foreign country, and have no pasta belly, no cultured friends, no Italian dreamboat of a man to romance me with fine dining and sparkling wine.

No Quinn.

My computer dings, announcing a new email. Wiping my tears with the sleeve of my cardigan, I pull myself up off the floor and peek at the screen.

My breath catches in my throat, and I almost fall out of my chair. It's an email from QKINGSLEY.

Subject: Checking in

Dearest Alessandra,

I hope the radio silence means that you're having so much fun, you've forgotten about your life back in Boston. Italy must be incredible. I hope it has swept you off your feet, or at least kept you well fed on delicious Italian cuisine and wine.

Boston is lifeless without you. Every Thursday, I wait for you to walk through the door, but am instead greeted by our old friend Sal. He senses that I miss you. I'm distracted, constantly staring out the window during our lessons. We talk mostly about you, in Italian, of course. The poor man has unwittingly become a sort of grief counselor for me. He says my Italian has improved, though. I said, only thanks to Alessandra.

It's not the same, however. The language has no flavor in my mouth any longer. It's dry, like sand, no longer rich and full of life. Sal has asked if I would like to continue lessons as he's afraid he can no longer teach me in this state. I will continue, don't worry. Quitting the language would only make me feel farther from you.

I'm sorry, I don't mean to bring down your spirits. I only mean to convey how very important you have become to me. I sincerely hope that Italy is everything you ever dreamed it would be, and more. I can't wait to hear about it. Soon, please.

With my utmost affection,

Quinn

Tears sting my eyes as I scramble for my phone. I don't care how much this will cost. I don't care that I'm six hours ahead of him. I need to speak to him, or even just leave a voice mail. I need to hear his voice.

The phone rings once.

"Alessandra?"

My name on his tongue is the sweetest sound—urgent and sweet at once. I almost begin to cry again, but swallow my tears.

"Quinn, hello. I—"

"You called. You finally called."

"Yes, I'm so sorry that I haven't yet. It must be so early."

"No, no, it's fine." He laughs. "I was awake. Been having trouble sleeping, actually."

"Me, too," I say, and my voice cracks a little.

"Are you all right?" He's so perceptive, always aware of my moods, even when I try to hide them.

"Of course. I'm just tired. It's been a whirlwind with work," I say, not completely lying.

"I'm sure, with all the people you're meeting, too."

I swallow a lump in my throat, taking in the bareness of my desolate flat. "Yes, it's so busy, but it's amazing." I don't even believe myself when I say it. How could he? There's silence on the other end. And then—

"I miss you," he says, his voice low.

"Me too," I whisper back, my heart fulfilled with so many conflicting emotions. "I miss you terribly."

"Tell me everything. Is your apartment okay? Is it everything you dreamed?"

I nod my head enthusiastically, hoping to quell the tears I can feel rising in my eyes. "It's wonderful. I woke up early yesterday and watched the sunrise. The food is incredible; you'd love it. I even bought myself a bike to get around."

"That sounds amazing."

"It's great," I say, forcing the words out.

"You'll call again?" he asks, the question almost an earnest command.

"Yes, I will." I close my eyes and savor these last few moments.

"Good. . .good." The relief in his voice fills my ear with such devotion, I can almost feel his thumb, gently running along the side of my face to push my stray hairs aside.

"*Talk soon*," I promise.

"*"Talk soon*."

We both sit in the silence of our shared misery for long, aching seconds. I stare at the screen, watching the seconds go by before I press a shaking finger on the END CALL button.

My tears fall freely now, slipping down my cheeks. This is a homesickness I could have never imagined.

What am I doing here?

Chapter Eighteen

Quinn

I hang up the phone and toss it onto my nightstand. Wide awake and restless, I stand and pace around my bedroom, my eyebrows scrunched together, my hands jittery at my sides. Alessandra said she was happy, said everything was fine. But the moment her words hit my ears? I could only think one thing.

She's lying.

Something's wrong. I could hear it in her voice, and I can sense it now in my gut. A slow, gnawing feeling tells me to call her back, to make her tell me what's going on.

I pick up my phone and immediately put it back down. She's lying for a reason. What would make her be honest with me now?

I continue pacing my room, the restlessness in my bones growing harder to ignore by the second. I have to do something. Any chance of being able to sleep was lost the moment Alessandra called. I have to do something. I have to help her. There's no way in hell I'm just going to sit here and pretend that nothing's going on.

Without thinking, I open a travel app on my phone. If I can look in her eyes, I'll know what's going on. I can only help her if I get her to tell me what's going on. And there's only one way to be sure that happens.

I have to fly to Rome as soon as possible—and there's something I can't forget to take with me.

• • •

During the entire flight to Italy, my mind is racing with worries about Alessandra. Why would she lie to me? What is she hiding? After all we've been through together, after how much we've shared. . .it breaks my heart to think she feels like she can't be honest.

Once we land, I take a taxi straight from the airport to Alessandra's apartment. I called Deanna to get her address before I left this morning. While Deanna seemed suspicious at first, once I told her what I had planned, she immediately agreed to help. Romantic at heart, I guess.

When the taxi pulls up in front of Alessandra's building, I get that strange fluttery feeling in my stomach again. No matter how badly I want to be annoyed with myself, I can't help but smile. I know what that feeling means now, and I stopped being afraid of it weeks ago.

I'm in love with her.

I step out of the taxi, my sleek carry-on in tow, and walk up to the doorway. Scanning the intercom system, I find 3C. I take a deep breath and hit the call button, holding the buzzer down for a solid three seconds before letting go. My stomach is tighter than ever. My limbs feel jittery, and I can't keep myself from grinning with excitement.

This is it. This is the moment. *Our* moment.

I know now why she was holding back, why she was afraid to be honest with me on the phone. I can't wait to see her, to sweep her up in my arms, to feel the supple curves of her body pressing against mine.

My thoughts are interrupted by the static buzz of the intercom.

"*Pronto,*" an unfamiliar Italian voice barks at me.

I furrow my brow. *I did hit 3C, right?*

I stammer out the words in Italian, unable to hide the

confusion in my voice. *I'm looking for Alessandra.*

"She's not here," the unfamiliar voice retorts.

My heart sinks. *Of course she's not here, you fucking idiot.*

"*Quando tornerà?*" I ask. *When will she be back?*

But the voice doesn't answer. I stand there in silence for a few moments before sighing and rubbing the back of my neck.

Stepping away from the doorstep and looking around, I notice the sign for the café next door. I go in, deciding to sit and wait for her there. It's not like there's anything else for me to do but wait.

I order a double espresso and take a seat near one of the front windows. *Thank God for those Italian lessons.* I knew they'd come in handy, but I didn't think I'd be putting them to use this soon.

As I settle into my seat, I slip my hand into my pocket, running my fingers over the smooth gold band of my mother's ring. My brothers and I were young when she died, and all these years, we've kept her most treasured possession tucked away, locked up in a box we never spoke of. It wasn't until we started dating more seriously that we remembered we still had our mother's ring. After two weeks of arguing, my brothers agreed that I should have it to give away—being the firstborn and all. It seems silly thinking about it now, but I'm glad my brothers left it to me. They're both happily married, those lucky little fuckers, and right now, I can use all the help I can get.

Out of the corner of my eye, I see a young couple approaching, laughing and joking in Italian. There's a slight glare through the window, so I can't quite see their faces, but from the sound of their laughter, they're having a good time. I can't quite hear what they're saying over the din of the café, but I don't need to—their body language says it all.

As they get closer, my stomach drops.

It's Alessandra. Having the time of her life with some other guy. An Italian guy. An attractive Italian guy.

Fuck.

I am such a fucking idiot. I never should have come here.

Clearly, I misread the situation. She's happy. She's moved on. I'm the loser who's been pining away every day since she left.

Fuck, fuck, fuck.

I quickly stand, desperate to get out of there and far away from Alessandra without her noticing. Gathering my things, I push my chair in and turn to leave, keeping my head down to keep her from seeing me. Just as I'm about to exit the café home-free, I run smack into an entering customer who yelps and berates me in Italian, yelling words I haven't learned yet, but can guess their meaning from the look on the man's face.

I mutter an apology as fast as I can while trying to get around him. But he blocks my way, stepping closer to me and yelling louder, until finally I'm able to push around him, exiting the café and walking briskly in the opposite direction of Alessandra.

Just as I think I've safely escaped, a familiar voice stops me dead in my tracks.

"Quinn?"

Fuck.

I stop and take a breath, bracing myself for the awkwardness about to happen. When I turn around,

Alessandra is only a few feet away from me, her mouth hanging open, her eyes wide with disbelief.

Even now, she's stunning. Her long, dark hair hangs loosely around her shoulders. Her hair is windblown, and her cheeks are rosy from walking around in the sunshine. But despite how happy she sounded earlier with the Italian guy, there's something in her face I don't recognize. A tinge that wasn't there in Boston. Sadness? Discomfort? I can't tell what it is, but it bothers me to see it.

I offer her a weak smile and she shakes her head.

"Wha-what are you doing here?"

I take a step backward, raising one hand in surrender. "I'm sorry. I shouldn't have come. It's clear now that you've moved on," I say, nodding to the Italian guy, who's now leaving on a moped.

Alessandra furrows her brow. "Antonio? No, he—I work with him. And his *fiancée*." She crosses her arms.

Thank fucking God.

"Oh, uh. I—it looked like…" I stammer, unsure how to explain my jealousy. But before I can form a full sentence, Alessandra closes the distance between us, a curious smile spreading across her lips.

"I've missed you," she says. When she rises on tiptoe to kiss my cheek, I relax at her touch, my cock suddenly stirring at the nearness of her ample curves. "Now, will you please tell me what the hell you're doing here?"

I sigh and shake my head. "On the phone. . .you just, you sounded so sad. I had to come and make sure you were okay."

Tears well in her eyes, and I can tell I've hit a nerve. I pull her into me, and she lays her head on my chest, so I can feel the warmth of her skin through my shirt. We hold each other for a few moments before Alessandra pulls away, wiping her eyes and letting out a small laugh.

She takes my hand in hers, nodding over her shoulder. "We should talk."

Chapter Nineteen

Alessandra

Quinn wraps his hand around mine as he leads me down the hall to our hotel room. There wouldn't be privacy in my flat with Flora, so I'm grateful he's brought me here. Plus, the idea of Quinn and Flora inhabiting the same space honestly makes me want to laugh. They are creatures from very different realities.

Looking at him out of the corner of my eye, I can say without a doubt that I prefer this reality. But is this real? I squeeze his hand, checking. A firm squeeze back quashes any doubts I have.

The quiet and contemplative taxi ride gave me plenty of time to overthink this moment, to change my mind and keep the divide between my life in the States and my life here clear. But with the lovely low lighting of this hotel and the smell of fragrant wines wafting through the air, I can't think of any reason why I should differentiate the two. After all, Quinn is here in Italy with me. *For* me. Even if it kills me all over again when he leaves, I need tonight. Need to feel whole again, desperately. And I do in his presence.

We take our time locating his room, wandering the halls in a comfortable silence that anticipates a full night of talking and reconnecting. There is no rush, there are no obligations. Once we enter this room, we step into the bubble of our shared bliss. I have no intention of leaving that bubble anytime soon, and by the way he leisurely runs his thumb across the back of my hand, I know he's on the same page as me.

The door clicks behind us as I take in the room before me. Curtains drape elegantly around a large window, teasing me with the promise of a view. I smile broadly and look at Quinn, knowing that my excitement must be written all over my face. He gives my hand another small squeeze before letting go. I walk to the window and pull the curtains aside. The sight before me is everything I dreamed of when I was back home. It was every magazine and brochure cut-out I tucked away for my dream life, my dream job, in this beautiful city.

A small balcony looks over the warmly lit square on which this little gem is located. People wander the streets, playing instruments, laughing, and chatting. I crack open the window a few inches, and the cool night air tickles my cheeks. I breathe it in, and a sense of calm washes over me like it hasn't since I arrived in this foreign country. I feel so safe in this hotel room, the world opening up again before me. Here, taking in this amazing view, there are no lousy stipends, no peanut-butter-thieving roommates. There's just me, this view, and—

Quinn leans against a wall behind me. I turn to him, sensing his distance.

"What are you doing over there?" I ask, curious.

He smiles. "Taking it all in." He's clearly staring at me, not the view.

I blush automatically and laugh at the cheesy line. He's as romantic as ever. That will never get old. I watch as he runs his thumb over the cork of a new bottle of champagne, a silent invitation to drink with him.

"Compliments of the hotel." He grins, his eyes sparkling. They're so soft and familiar, like a blanket I want to never, ever fall from my shoulders.

"*Come here*," I say, urgently reaching for his free hand. "And bring that with you." I eye the champagne with a smirk.

"Yes, ma'am," he says with mock seriousness.

I love that he plays these games with me. *God,* I've missed this. I've missed *him.* It's only been two weeks since I last saw him, but it could have been lifetimes, I've missed him so much.

My heart swells as Quinn's hand finds mine, closing the distance between us. I pull him to me, wanting to occupy the same space as him. His eyes are darker now, glittering in the evening glow of the square. I want to kiss him. I run my thumb across his knuckles, lifting my other hand to his perfectly carved jawline. Just one little kiss—

"Shall we take a moment first?" He stops me, catching my fingers against his lips with a gentle kiss. Sensing my reaction, he says, "I only think that if you kiss me, I may not be able to stop. I'd like to hear about your life here first. You need your mouth for speaking. You see my conundrum?"

"I do." I nod my head. "And I would agree, but I have yet to give you a proper welcome to Italy." I smile, pulling him back in for that exquisite taste before he can resist me any longer.

My lips press against him with a relief that I can't describe. He sighs against them. I know he feels it, too, the way his mouth melts into mine. I hear the soft thump of the champagne bottle as he tosses it on the bed.

Now both of his hands are free. They immediately find the contours of my cheeks, holding my face to his as if I'm a precious treasure. The breeze from the open window wraps around us in a cool embrace, inviting us to move even closer as we yearn for the refuge of each other's arms. The feeling is sublime.

We break apart, forehead resting against forehead, soul against soul.

"There. Do you feel welcomed?" I ask, looking up at him through my lashes.

He runs his thumb across my lower lip. "I'm fairly new to the area. I may need more reacquainting."

Quinn captures my mouth in another kiss, this time demanding my lips to part beneath his. His tongue flicks forward to meet mine in a hungry search. It's obvious that we both have two weeks of pent-up longing, two weeks of missing this, and put every emotion, every moment of desire for the other, into this kiss. His breath is hot on my mouth, and I moan into the kiss. I dig my fingers into his firm shoulders, pulling myself as close to him as I can manage.

"God, Alessandra," he says softly against the corner of my mouth, giving me a moment to catch my breath. He kisses a trail down the side of my neck, dipping me back for more leverage. I let him hold me up, knowing that even if I were to fall completely limp to his need, he wouldn't let me go. He'd catch me and keep me, protect me from everything outside of this bubble we've surrounded ourselves with.

I breathe the scent of his hair in as he kisses down my sternum. This is real, isn't it? Quinn is really here, in Italy, showering me with the most adoring kisses. I have an exquisite view from the window before us, but it doesn't compare to the sensations of smell, touch, and taste I have with this man in my arms. Nothing can compare.

Quinn is on his knees before me, gently kissing down my body. I'm drunk with want, raking my hands through his thick hair and down his back. He runs his hands across every surface of me. From my arms to my back, my waist to my thighs. I lower myself to my knees, drawing his face to meet mine for another needy kiss. Together, we unbutton each other's clothes. . .my fingers deftly undoing his pants, and his gently pulling down the zipper of my dress.

I unbuckle his pants while sucking on his lower lip, drawing it between my teeth. He moans from deep in his throat, his desire for me evident by the firm, hard cock now throbbing in my hand. His hands reach deftly up under my dress, finding the silken edge of my panties and pulling them down.

We shed the rest of our clothes and fall onto the bed.

Quinn's hands run up and down my body, one to my breast, worshipping the nipple, massaging the fullness of it. I take over, my want outweighing any premise of taking our time, and climb on top of him, positioning him at my entrance. His eyes meet mine as I slowly sink down.

Two weeks of my body missing him means I have to stretch for his girth, but I do so with eager thrusts.

Staring deeply into each other's eyes, I can tell neither

of us is going to last. It's been too long since we've felt each other. It's too powerful. This moment. Me, him, here. Too good.

Quinn pushes himself up easily into a sitting position as I continue to ride him, my legs now wrapped intimately around his waist. With one firm arm, he draws one of my legs up slightly, changing the angle so he can thrust even deeper than I thought possible. I gasp, my heel now digging into the center of his back, my toes curling.

He pulls aside my long, dark hair and presses his mouth against my ear. "*Ti amo*, Alessandra. *Ti amo.*" *I love you.*

My orgasm hits me like an explosion of warm light, starting low and rippling through my every molecule with electric energy. He thrusts through the waves of it, moaning with every contraction. With a final, needy kiss, Quinn follows me, his own climax washing over him.

● ● ●

"So that has been my living nightmare," I say, finishing the story of my latest run-in with Flora's very public sex life.

Quinn takes a moment to digest the image I've painted for him. He shakes his head, taking a gulp of his champagne. "I'm sorry it hasn't been everything you'd dreamed." He sighs, eyeing his empty glass.

I feel light from the champagne. Or maybe it's having him by my side. I'm not sure.

We haven't bothered to dress, aside from a pair of boxer shorts for him and a tank top and panties for me. We ordered room service—more wine, and some cheese, bread, and pasta.

After answering the door in the hotel robes, we're now comfortable again on the bed.

I laugh at Quinn's enthusiasm to uncork the bottle of red wine. With his hair mussed and his cheeks lightly flushed in the soft light of the rising sun, he looks younger than ever.

He pours me a little wine before tasting his own. The way his lips curl around his glass in a smirk makes me want to fuck him all over again.

Instead, I indulge another way by taking a hearty bite of delicious penne, soaked in olive oil and herbs. He plants a kiss on my forehead before standing and walking over to his bag. He takes out a pair of pants and begins to put them on.

"Um, please don't tell me you're going somewhere," I say, disbelieving.

He seems genuinely appalled by the idea. "Where in God's name would I go?"

"Then why do you need pants?"

He pauses his belt buckling with a thoughtful frown. "Point taken."

Quinn whips off his belt and takes off his pants again, throwing them into our little nest. I throw back my head and laugh—really, truly laugh. Our bodies find each other again, nestling close.

"It's almost dawn," I say, looking out the window, drawing the blanket closer around us. "Did I really talk all night?"

"I've talked as much as listened," he reminds me.

"Yes. I'm glad you've made so many strides in finding your brother. That's truly incredible. I'm so excited for you," I murmur, feeling the emotion percolate in the moisture of my eyes.

"Are you crying?" He chuckles and plants a kiss on my temple. "It's all thanks to you I even looked for him."

"Oh, stop. *Ti amo.*" The words leap out of me in a happy sigh. I don't try to stop them. Why would I? We both know it's true.

"*Ti amo,*" he whispers in my ear. *I love you.*

A colossal tear falls from my cheek. "God, I'm sorry. I'm crying all over y—"

As I look for where the unruly tear must have landed, my words halt in my throat. There, in his hand, rests a ring. A simple golden band shining in the low light.

"Alessandra," he says, lifting my chin with his other hand. His eyes search mine. "Marry me."

Marry him?

Quinn Kingsley wants to marry me.

"We can stay here," he says. "I have the means to provide for a life for you here and in the States. We'll have two homes. I'd do anything to build a home with you.

What do you say?"

For the first time since meeting this man, through every bilingual conversation, every cute quip, every whispered sweet nothing—I have no words. All I can do is nod *yes, yes, yes,* choking back tears.

"Is that a—"

I cut him off with a crushing kiss. He sighs against my lips, drawing me close against his perfect warmth.

Yes, Quinn Kingsley.. A thousand times, yes.

Chapter Twenty

Quinn

"Buongiorno, amore mio." Good morning, my love.

I wake to Alessandra's voice whispering in my ear, which brings a smile to my face. My cock immediately stirs to life.

I turn over to find her curled up next to me, her lips already forming into a pout at the small distance I've made between us by rolling over. With a grin, I pull her to me, relishing in the feeling of her skin against my bare chest, the soft movements her body makes when she breathes. I place a kiss on her forehead, and she turns her face to mine. Even now, after everything we've been through, after thinking I'd lost her only to find her again, my stomach tightens when she looks at me like that.

You're one lucky fucker, Kingsley.

"Buongiorno," I reply, moving my hand down her back and resting it on her perfect ass.

Alessandra raises her eyebrows, drawing circles on

my chest with her fingertips in response.

"How is my *bellissima* fiancée this morning?"

"*Perfecto*," she purrs, entwining her legs with mine and resting her head on my shoulder.

If I wasn't exhausted from the marathon fucking we did last night, I would be making a move on her right now.

When I flew here, my one plan in Italy was to win Alessandra back and make her my fiancée. Now that that's been done? I didn't see the harm in the two of us sticking around here for a while, and I even cleared it with my brothers, who are happy to run the business in my absence for a little while.

Alessandra and I spent the past week traveling all over the country. We rode Vespas through Tuscany, walked on the beach in Capri, visited just about every museum and church in Rome, climbed to the top of the Duomo in Florence, and went shopping in Milan. Every day together has been a new adventure, eating and drinking and laughing and kissing and fucking. It's been perfect. If it weren't for our double-espresso shots every morning, I don't think we'd have the energy to make it through the day.

We take our time getting ready for today's adventure, lounging in bed until our stomachs prompt us to find food. We throw some clothes on, brush our teeth, and head for the café next to her apartment—the same café where she found me the day I first got here.

After ordering our espressos and pastries, we grab a small table in the corner, sitting close enough that our knees touch under the table.

"So, my fiancé, what's the plan for the day?" Alessandra winks, flipping her long, dark braid over her shoulder.

"We're going to the Sabine Hills." I smile.

"Mmm, sounds fancy. What will we do there?"

"I signed us up for a vineyard tour. . .and I might have pulled a few strings to get us a private cooking lesson with one of the most sought-after chefs in the region."

Alessandra's smile fades, shock taking its place. "You're joking."

"No jokes, *signorina*. I thought you'd enjoy it."

"Quinn, oh, my God!" She squeals, making everyone else in the café stare at us.

I can't keep myself from smiling. I love it when I impress her, and I love it even more when she gets excited like that.

"Sorry," she mutters, quickly hiding her face in her hands.

"Don't be." I chuckle. "I'm just glad you're excited."

"Of course I'm excited, are you kidding? The love of my life whisking me around Italy, making me feel like a freaking princess?" Her enthusiasm causes a few other customers to give us dirty looks, and she quickly ducks her head to hide her face again.

We quickly finish our pastries and make our way to the train station, eager to begin our adventure.

Once we arrive at the Sabine Hills, Alessandra and I are both overwhelmed by how beautiful the scenery is. I knew it was going to be pretty, but the view we are met with? It's better than I ever could have imagined.

Lush greenery is everywhere, stretching as far as the eye can see. Rows and rows of vines line the hillside, and the buildings look like castles straight out of a storybook. Alessandra and I take it all in in silence, our fingers interlaced as we walk slowly toward the vineyard.

When we find the main building, we're greeted by a middle-aged man with curly hair and a toothy smile who throws his hands in the air when he sees us.

"Welcome, my friends. My name is Niccolo, and I'll be leading your tour today."

Niccolo and I shake hands, and he brings Alessandra's fingers to his mouth, giving them a quick peck. Alessandra turns to me and arches an eyebrow.

"Better look out, Quinn. I'll expect you to greet me like he did all the time now," she says with a wink.

We all laugh as Niccolo gestures for us to follow him, turning and leading us down the hallway into a darker, stone-walled room with various wine-making tools and machines. With my arm around Alessandra, the two of us follow Niccolo and listen politely while he explains how wine is made.

Once he's finished explaining all the tools in this room, he leads us into the next one, which looks about the same, only with large wooden barrels instead of tools. Plus, this one smells a lot more like fermenting grapes. Niccolo tells us about all the different kinds of wine they make here, as well as the special certifications they're required to go through.

With each new wine he describes, Niccolo hands us a generous sample. Less than a full glass, but definitely enough for multiple sips. Alessandra and I tip our glasses together each time, unable to contain our contentment with simply being together.

As the tour goes on and the wine continues to pour, Alessandra and I grow more and more affectionate. In the back of my mind, part of me knows that we're pretty much acting like a couple of teenagers. But the rest of my mind? It's really fucking in love with my fiancée and simply doesn't care.

We wrap our arms around each other and steal kisses every chance we get. Hell, in the fifteen minutes of free time we had between the winery tour and the cooking lesson, I considered sneaking off for a quickie in the cellar. But, hey, even I have limits. Even when I'm this wildly, passionately, insanely in love.

When it's time for our cooking lesson, Niccolo leads us to a rustic kitchen overlooking the rolling hills below, where he introduces us to Chef Giovanni, our teacher for the day.

"*Benvenuto.*" Chef Giovanni welcomes us, his broad smile making his already rosy cheeks a little rosier. He asks if we're hungry, and Alessandra and I turn and smile at each other.

"*Sì,*" I reply, slipping my arm around Alessandra's shoulders. *We're very hungry.*

Alessandra chimes in, adding that we're ready to learn.

Chef Giovanni raises his eyebrows playfully, chuckling at our eagerness. "*Tu parli italiano?*" *You speak Italian?*

"She speaks Italian," I say, rubbing Alessandra's shoulder and kissing her forehead.

"*È un bravo studente.*" She giggles, patting my shoulder. *He's a good student.*

Chef Giovanni smiles and raises an eyebrow, giving us an appraising look. "Are you lovers?" he asks as he pulls a slab of mozzarella from a tub and begins slicing it into thick pieces.

Alessandra blushes, looking down at her feet to hide her embarrassment.

"*Sì*," I reply, placing my fingers under Alessandra's chin to lift her face to mine. We kiss slowly and tenderly. It may be the wine, or it may be us, but the kiss builds in urgency, so much so that I feel a stirring, prompting me to pull away.

Down, boy.

Giovanni seems unfazed by our very public display of affection. Instead of being embarrassed, he offers us wishes for a happy life together.

"*Grazie*," we reply together, unable to hide our happiness.

"Well, let's begin," Chef Giovanni says.

To begin our cooking lesson, he lectures us on how to properly pair wines and cheeses, giving us plenty of samples of each. He then teaches us how to make a perfect pizza, handmade pasta, and perfectly seasoned chicken. The food is amazing, and I can't help but be impressed with how quickly Alessandra picks up Chef Giovanni's techniques.

Every time I think I know this woman, she teaches me something new about herself. Every second I spend with her here confirms the one thought that's been bouncing around in my head since she said yes to my proposal.

I'm one lucky bastard.

After our cooking lesson ends, we pack up the leftovers from our meal and say good-bye to our guides for the day.

"*Grazie*, Chef Giovanni. This was wonderful," I say, reaching out to shake the chef's hand.

"*Prego, prego*," Giovanni replies, taking my hand between both of his and shaking vigorously.

Alessandra thanks him as well, and the two of us make our way down the path to the train station.

"Good-bye, American lovers!" Niccolo yells from the terrace. He waves heartily, and Alessandra and I stop to turn and wave back. "Come again—and bring your friends!"

We nod and wave good-bye again before turning to walk to the station.

"That's a good idea, actually," Alessandra says, lacing her fingers through mine. "We should come back and bring your brothers along next time. They'd love it here."

I turn and smile at my fiancée. "You're right. They'd love it here. Maybe the Forbidden Desires executive team will have to have their annual retreat in the Sabine Hills next year."

"Wives are welcome too, though, right?"

"Hmm. . .I don't know about that." I stroke my chin and raise an eyebrow.

"Quinn!" She elbows me in the ribs, slightly harder than she means to. I think.

"Hey, watch it! You're stronger than you think, you know?" I say, rubbing my side.

"Yeah, well. For a while there, I thought I'd be doing all this alone. A girl's gotta be able to watch out for herself."

Taking her hand in mine, I pull her closer to me. "Well, you don't have to do it alone anymore. I'm here now. Always."

On the train ride back to Rome, Alessandra curls up next to me in her seat, resting her head on my shoulder.

"Don't fall asleep," I murmur, turning to kiss her softly.

"I won't." She sighs, her eyes already fluttering closed.

As the train rumbles along, I look out the window, watching the Italian countryside roll by. Alessandra's breathing grows slow and deep, and the full weight of her head presses into me. Draping her cardigan over her shoulders, I pull her close. She murmurs softly, readjusting and settling into me.

With the love of my life by my side and the Italian countryside out the window, I can't believe that this is my life. That everything worked out the way it did, so that the two of us can be together.

It's almost like it was all meant to be.

Epilogue

Alessandra

"Come in, come in." I usher Gavin and Emma inside. Upon returning from Italy, I moved into Quinn's penthouse apartment, and amazingly, it already feels like home.

Emma is positively glowing, and Gavin is too—his mood has changed ever since they announced they were expecting. Only a faint hint is visible beneath her sweater, and I can't wait to see how adorable she is with a real baby bump. Over the past few months, Emma and Corinne have both adopted me into the fold, and I feel like I've become part of the Kingsley family already.

Emma gives me a quick hug, and Gavin squeezes my hand. "Where have you been hiding that grumpy brother of mine?" he asks.

Quinn isn't a grump. At least, not anymore, and especially not with me, but I chuckle at Gavin anyway.

"We've been busy with wedding planning," I say, leading them into the dining room.

The weekly Sunday dinners became sporadic over the last couple of months since we returned from Italy after an extended vacation and threw ourselves into wedding-planning mode. Quinn has been exceedingly helpful, and though I never expected to do it all alone, I've been amazed at how involved he is. From picking flowers to deciding on our color scheme, he's been right there every step of the way.

Cooper and Corinne are already seated in the dining room, and Corinne's lifelong childhood friend, Aaron, is here, too, currently looking at the aquarium in Quinn's study from his wheelchair.

I sit down to chat with the girls while Gavin and Cooper join Quinn in the kitchen. He still won't accept much help, as he loves to cook for his family, but I know they're not discussing his roasting techniques for the prime rib he's serving. The conversations these past few weeks have been dominated by the topic of the Kingsleys' long-lost brother, Will. A couple of weeks ago, Quinn succeeded in tracking him down, and the brothers all met for coffee as a sort of get-to-know-you meeting. They've since met for dinner and are working on building a relationship.

I'm so happy that it was my encouragement that led Quinn to pursue finding out more about his family. I know it pains him to think that he won't have family to attend our wedding—other than his brothers, of course—but the excitement of finding a new family member has been a good distraction.

"So, six more weeks until the big day," Corinne says, smiling at me with genuine happiness.

"I know. I can hardly believe it."

"And everything's on track with the planning?" Emma asks.

I nod. "I just need to complete my final dress fitting."

With Quinn's money and influence pulling the strings, all the wedding service providers from churches to reception venues to florists were all very accommodating with us. It also helps that I no longer work full-time as a nanny, which means I have time to devote to getting all of our affairs squared away.

My plan was to tutor students studying Italian and just enjoy life with my new husband. But Quinn's thinking was if I was tied to a full-time job, I wouldn't be able to pick up and take off with him on business trips or vacations, and I wasn't going to argue.

I hear the men finish their hushed conversation, and Quinn leads the pack into the dining room, carrying a large platter of meat.

"That looks amazing," I say as he sets it in the center of the table. I spent the hour before our guests arrived preparing the side dishes alongside my amazing fiancé, and see that each brother is carrying a dish—whipped potatoes and roasted vegetables.

Corinne brings Aaron and we all take our places at the table.

"I feel like a goddess with our men serving us," Emma says, chuckling.

Gavin presses a kiss to the top of her hair. "You are a goddess," he murmurs. "My goddess."

"Oh, the wine," I say, noticing the empty glasses at each placesetting.

"Let's open one of the bottles we brought back from our favorite vineyard in Italy," Quinn suggests. His gaze finds mine and we share a secret smile.

I follow him into the kitchen, where he backs me up against the counter and steals a kiss that takes my breath away. His muscular frame holds me in place while his warm tongue slides over mine.

"*Bellissima,*" he whispers against my lips.

"They'll see us," I whisper back.

"Hmm, don't care," he murmurs before kissing me deeply once again. His fingers intertwine with mine, and I can feel the press of my ring against the palm of his hand.

My engagement ring had been a simple gold band belonging to Quinn's mother, up until about two weeks ago. He took me to the big fancy jewelry store downtown and told me to pick out a diamond to have mounted to the ring. After perusing my options, I opted for a three-carat solitaire. My new ring is actually his mother's ring melted down and formed into a sturdy new band that holds the diamond. I absolutely love it. It's new and old at the same time, and holds such sentimental value for Quinn, which makes me even more honored to wear it.

When I remember how he teared up the first time he

saw the ring on my finger, a lump forms in my throat, and I fold myself into his warm embrace.

Quinn pulls back slowly, his eyes finding mine. "*Ti amo,*" he whispers in perfect Italian.

"I love you, too."

"Let's go," he says, and I follow my amazing fiancé back to the table to enjoy the feast he's prepared for our family.

Get the Next Book

To ensure you don't miss Kendall Ryan's next book, sign up and you'll get a release-day reminder.

www.kendallryanbooks.com/newsletter

Up Next

Bro Code

There's pretty much only one rule when you're a guy.

Don't be a douche.

Turns out, the fastest way to break that rule is to fall for your best friend's sister.

Ava's brilliant, sharp-tongued, gorgeous, and ten years younger than me.

She's the sexual equivalent of running with scissors. In a word, she's dangerous. And completely off-limits.

Falling for her could ruin everything.

Yet I can't seem to stop, even when her company is threatened by a lawsuit, and my promotion hinges on representing the opposing client—and winning.

I can't see a way out of this mess that doesn't end in a broken friendship, a broken heart, or a ruined career.

I may have broken the bro code when I fell for Ava. But do I have the balls to handle what comes next?

Acknowledgments

I would thank to offer so many thanks to the beautiful readers who have followed this series, beginning with Gavin's story in *Dirty Little Secret*. I threw myself into the world of Forbidden Desires, and the Kingsley brothers have dominated my time and all my waking thoughts for the past eight months. I really hope you enjoyed their stories as much as I have. *Grazie*!

Connect with Kendall

Website

www.kendallryanbooks.com/

Facebook

www.facebook.com/kendallryanbooks

Twitter

www.twitter.com/kendallryan1

Instagram

www.instagram.com/kendallryan1

Newsletter

www.kendallryanbooks.com/newsletter/

About the Author

A *New York Times*, *Wall Street Journal*, and *USA TODAY* bestselling author of more than two dozen titles, Kendall Ryan has sold over two million books, and her books have been translated into several languages in countries around the world. Her books have also appeared on the *New York Times* and *USA TODAY* bestseller list more than three dozen times. Kendall has been featured in publications such as *USA TODAY*, *Newsweek*, and *In Touch Magazine*. She lives in Texas with her husband and two sons.

Other Books by Kendall Ryan

Unravel Me

Make Me Yours

Working It

Craving Him

All or Nothing

When I Break Series

Filthy Beautiful Lies Series

The Gentleman Mentor

Sinfully Mine

Bait & Switch

Slow & Steady

The Room Mate

The Play Mate

The House Mate

The Bed Mate

The Soul Mate

Hard to Love

Reckless Love

Resisting Her

The Impact of You

Screwed

Monster Prick

The Fix Up

Sexy Stranger

Dirty Little Secret

Dirty Little Promise

Torrid Little Affair

xo, Zach

Baby Daddy

For a complete list of Kendall's books, visit:

www.kendallryanbooks.com/all-books/